PUMPKIN Spice and not so Nice

By Becky Monson

Other Books by Becky

Thirty-Two Going on Spinster
Thirty-Three Going on Girlfriend
Thirty-Four Going on Bride
Speak Now or Forever Hold Your Peace
Taking a Chance
Once Again in Christmas Falls
Just a Name
Just a Girl
The Accidental Text
The Love Potion
How to Ruin the Holidays

Connect with Becky

www.beckymonson.com

To my Grandma M.
I'm sad you won't get to read this one.
I'll miss your spunky attitude and quick wit.
Love you always.

Chapter One

Jenna Peterson's Guide to Dating Emotionally Unavailable Men:

When dating an emotionally unavailable man, get ready for disappointment. Because there's going to be a lot of it.

Well, I guess that settles it. I'm cursed.
There's no other explanation for it.

Along with their parents,
Cameron Wade Jacobsen
and
Kaytlynn Elizabeth Bristow
Are pleased to announce . . .

Another wedding invitation for another ex-boyfriend's nuptials. There have been four over the last year. Matthew, Brian, Garrett, and now Cam. This one from Cam has peonies on it—my favorite flower. And it's in Cabo. I've always dreamed of a destination wedding. It's like pouring salt in a wound and then squeezing some lemon juice on it for good measure.

Why am I cursed? Because for each and every one of those invites, I was the last person the grooms dated before they met their one true love, or . . . *whatever*. I don't even know if I buy into that "one true love" crap. How can there be only one person out there for you? What if you never run into that person? What if they die before you meet them? Can there be a second-best true love? Or third best, even?

Anyway, the point is, for all those men, I was *not* their one true love. I was the one before the true love, which makes me a pre-love. The rehearsal love. The *before* true love. Not that any of them ever said the word *love*. I've never had those three words, in that order, said to me. Unless you count old Frank at the deli counter I frequent. He says it all the time.

I shouldn't have opened the invite. I knew what it was when I hurriedly grabbed the small stack of letters from my mailbox this morning and scanned through it on the way to my car to drive to my family's farm, where I should have been fifteen minutes ago.

It was third in the stack. The clean white linen envelope with my address done up in handwritten calligraphy. I instantly felt that all-too-familiar feeling of dread circling around at the bottom of my belly. Even though I'd seen the Instagram posts. I'd seen the progression of Cam and Kaytlynn's relationship. I'd seen the over-the-top proposal. I knew the wedding was coming.

As with the three previous invites, I hadn't expected to be invited. I guess by now I should expect it, but I was once again surprised.

So, I did what I had to do: I tossed it and the rest of the mail into my purse and pushed this all off on Later Today Jenna. She could deal with it.

Except now here we are, later today. And Later Today Jenna doesn't want to deal with any of this.

"Whatcha got there?" Josie, my best friend and cousin, asks as she enters the small orange building near the entrance to the farm, where I spend most of my weekends during the months of September and October selling tickets to the largest pumpkin patch in the state of Nevada and chatting up the residents of Carson City, where our family farm has been for decades.

I'm in my normal weekend attire: an orange T-shirt with *Peterson's Pumpkin Patch* in white letters on the front and a pair of jeans I don't mind getting dirty. The orange beret with the little green stem that comes out the top is sitting on the counter by the computer. It's part of the uniform, but I try to take it off as much as possible.

I reach up to touch my grandma's gold band, which I wear on a chain around my neck, and then let out a breath. "Oh, you know," I say, waving the stationery around in the air. "Just another wedding invite."

Josie cocks her head to the side, breathing out her nose. "Jenna . . ."

"Nope," I cut her off with a wave of my hand. "No teacher face from you."

She crinkles her brow. "Teacher face?"

"Yes, you've got your teacher face on." She's always done it, but this is the first time I've called her out on it.

"I do not," she says, indignantly. Punctuating each word as her brow moves downward.

3

"Yes, you do." I point to her face. Josie is a third-grade teacher at Highland Academy, a private elementary school with a waiting list so long, it might actually be easier to get a Birkin bag. "You do this head tilt, high brows, and wide eyes thing." I make a little circular motion with my finger. "That, and it's kinda hard to take sympathy from someone in a pumpkin costume."

She huffs out a breath, trying to school her features as she fluffs out the large pumpkin shape covering her from her neck to just above her knees. An orange beanie atop her head, orange-and-black striped tights, and green felt shoes complete the look that was made by her mom — my aunt Lottie. Well, everything but the tights. We get those from Amazon.

She's Priscilla Pumpkin every year at Peterson's Pumpkin Patch, donning the costume and telling her adorable original stories to bright-eyed children and their parents. It's become part of the fall tradition, and we Petersons would be nothing without our traditions — the stemmed berets the rest of us wear during the season being one of them. Though I'd rather have Josie's beanie, the berets are actually one of the more benign traditions, to be honest. Some are so strange Josie and I have had to bend over backward to keep them strictly within the family. Like the pumpkin chant on the season's opening day. No need for everyone to see *all* our crazy.

"Stop trying to change the subject," Josie says, her teacher face now settling into a very knowing look.

Oh, right. I can't use that trick on her. She knows me better than anyone on the planet, since we've known each other our entire lives. We were even born three days apart and in the same hospital. First Josie, then me. She's tried before to pull rank as the older cousin, but it doesn't carry much weight.

4

It was all planned, of course, by our crazy, ridiculously intertwined families. Our moms are sisters, and our dads are brothers. Which makes us . . . some kind of strange double cousins. Oh, the jokes that were made at our expense in high school. I took them in stride, even adding a few of my own just to show they didn't hurt me. Sticks and stones and all that. For Josie, it only added to her high school drama. Which was a lot.

Our moms — who Josie and I refer to as "the sisters" — planned out their pregnancies so we'd all be close in age and the best of friends. It worked out for Josie and me, but not so much for my older sister, Olivia, and Josie's older brother, Oliver, who, despite the sisters trying, ended up being a year apart and *do not* get along. And yes, the names are on purpose. Oliver and Olivia, and Jenna and Josie. Just . . . *adorable*.

Anyway, it doesn't matter that Oliver and Olivia don't get along — they're still the favorites of the Peterson offspring. They have produced grandchildren, after all. And Josie and me? Well, we're the family disappointments. The black sheep.

I don't need anyone to be disappointed in me. I've got that covered all by myself. I had much bigger ideas about how my life should have turned out by now.

I huff out a breath. "Fine," I say as I wave the invite around. "It's from Cam." I slouch in my seat, letting my shoulders drop to emphasize how I feel about it.

She gives me a sad smile, her head starting to tilt again in that teacher way of hers before she quickly straightens it, catching herself this time. "I'm sorry, Jen." She holds out a hand, and I give her the invite.

"Peonies," she says at first glance. She looks to me with a poignant eyebrow raise before her eyes move back to the card.

"Yep," I say on an exhale.

5

She gasps and shakes her head. "Why would they spell *Kaytlynn* like that? So many *y*'s. I just can't with these weird spellings. Don't parents know how hard it is on teachers?"

I'd noticed that too. But was trying not to be petty.

While she continues to read, I busy my hands by grabbing the donation jar that sits near the register. I reach in and grab a wad of cash so I can begin the arduous task of separating and counting.

Peterson's Pumpkin Patch has never asked for donations before, that I know of. But the barn that burned down last year proved to be too much for my family to pay for, and insurance only covered half. I've been amazed at the people's kindness this year. We're three weeks into the season and we're halfway to our goal already. Even so, it's going to take a miracle to meet it.

Josie sets the invite on the counter. "Are you going?"

"No way," I say, setting the pile of money I was sorting aside and turning my head toward her.

"Good call. It's in Cabo. Only douchey people have destination weddings." The corner of her mouth pulls upward.

I let out a little snort. She knows all about my destination wedding dreams.

"That's the fourth one," I say with a nod toward the piece of cardstock.

She lets out a long breath. "I'm sorry."

I pull my chin inward and glare at my cousin. "I doubt you're sorry Cam is getting married to someone else."

Josie gives me a sheepish grin. "Um . . . no." She pulls the beanie off her head and runs her hands through her auburn hair, fluffing it up where it's matted to her head. "I won't miss Cam. But I'm sorry he broke your heart."

She wasn't alone in her feelings; the whole family hated Cam. They also didn't like Brian, Garrett, or Matthew. So basically, any of the last four boyfriends I've been daring enough to bring home.

It's probably hard for anyone to introduce significant others to family, because family can be extra judgy. As if no one can ever measure up. But with the Petersons, it's doubly hard. We're all close, but not like those lovey-dovey families you see on those cheesy shows. We're close in a super dysfunctional way. Like, all up in each other's business. And when we don't like someone, we aren't quiet about it. Like when Josie's brother, Oliver, met his wife, Kitty. None of us were sure about her at first, but now none of us are sure why she stays with him, but we're grateful she does. And then there's my sister Olivia's husband, Reginald Gilbert. None of us liked him at first and . . . well, we still can't stand him. But she married him anyway. She's always been so stubborn.

"You know," Josie starts, trying to put her hands on her hips but unable to do it properly through the puffiness of the pumpkin costume. She gives up and lets them hang at her sides. "I don't understand why these guys all invite you to their weddings. It's kinda weird. Trevor better not invite me to his wedding with Brenda." She does a full-body shiver.

"Ew," I say, scrunching my nose. "If he does, we'll have to go just so I can kick him in the nads."

Josie lets out a laugh at that. "You'd be my favorite person ever."

Trevor was Josie's ex-fiancé who called off the wedding, leaving her with a bunch of debt she'd accrued while planning said wedding, only to get engaged three months later to Brenda, his administrative assistant.

7

Of course, Trevor won't invite her to the wedding because that relationship ended with them in mediation over the ring. You know, the ring he wanted back so he could give it to *Brenda*. What a turd.

The last four relationships I've been in have ended in a very adult, kind manner. Definitely no mediation. Not even a big fight, now that I think of it. No yelling or screaming. It's always just been a conversation, and I've never been totally caught off guard by it. Like my subconscious had been expecting it. And every single one of them always had lovely things to say about me. Stuff like: *You made me see things I hadn't seen before. You've helped me so much. I'm a different man because of you. I can never thank you enough. But you just aren't enough for me.*

None of them actually said the last part. But it was implied. Because if all those things were true, then why didn't it work out with at least one of them?

I worked so hard on each of those relationships. Investing time getting them to open up, to give them the opportunity to talk about themselves and what was on their minds. It's a gift of mine. Or maybe more of a toxic trait. My toxic trait is that people tend to open up to me. It's like I have a sign on my head that says, *Dump your problems on Jenna!* Which makes me a magnet for emotionally unavailable men. Like flies on rotting fruit. I'm the rotting fruit in this metaphor, in case that wasn't obvious.

This is how it works for me: I meet a man. He's emotionally unavailable. I'm instantly attracted to said man. We start dating. I help him explore his emotions because of aforementioned gift and/or toxic trait. He feels his feelings, tells me how important I am in his life, and then breaks up with me. Then he takes his newfound emotionally open existence and finds the woman of his dreams and they live happily ever after.

Do those other women even know how lucky they are to have me? I'm looking at you, Kaytlynn with all the *y*'s. You're welcome.

I guess what it really comes down to is that I wasn't the right girl for any of them. Maybe someday I can attract an emotionally unavailable man that I am right for. Oh, to dream. Or maybe I should look for an emotionally *available* man next time.

Or maybe I should just give up on men entirely. It's not like they're knocking down my door. It's been over a year since I've been on a date with someone I'd be willing to go on a second date with.

I'm most definitely not going to entertain thoughts about Mr. Hot Doctor who sometimes works at the spa where I'm employed. He's just the kind of guy I attract. No more of that. I'm swearing off those kinds of men. I'll just spend the rest of my life living vicariously through the Turkish dramas Josie and I are obsessed with. Can Yaman, you have my heart.

"You okay?" Josie pulls me from my thoughts, giving me teacher face as she looks me over with her Peterson-green eyes — the same ones I have. All the Peterson offspring have the same green eyes. Neither me and Olivia nor Josie and Oliver got our moms' eyes. Those Peterson genes are strong. I did get my hair color from my mom. If only I'd inherited Josie's envy-worthy auburn color. *If only.* Instead, I have to spend a lot of money to keep highlights in my naturally mousy-brown locks.

"I'm fine," I say, not sounding fine at all. "I think what I need is a distraction." I look up at Josie and give her my best puppy dog eyes.

"Oh no," she says, shaking her head at me. "Last time you needed a distraction, I ended up in the hayfield driving a tractor around in my underwear."

I smile wistfully. "That was one of my better dares."

"The sisters didn't think so."

"They always ruin our fun," I say, and not facetiously. Our moms really are the ruiners of joy. "No, what I mean is I need a Jo Jo sleepover." *Jo Jo* is what her brother Oliver's three-year-old son, Charlie, had started calling Josie, and we've all taken to it.

In truth, I'm going to need a much bigger distraction to get my mind off all the men in my life—or rather ex-men—but spending some one-on-one time with Josie will be perfect for now. And anyway, I've missed my Josie time. Since I moved from Carson City to the mountain town of Aspen Lake, which is thirty minutes away but closer to work for me, we've been together less and less. Plus, I don't really feel like driving home tonight.

Josie's lips twist to the side. "I have that dinner I have to go to."

"Oh yes," I say, giving her a double eyebrow raise. I forgot she was going on a nondate-date. It's complicated. "Go get your freak on."

"There'll be none of that happening."

"Sure," I say, drawing out the word.

She shakes her head at me. "Just go hang at my place and I'll meet you there after dinner, okay? I'll be ready to party it up when I get back. Don't burn Cam's wedding invitation without me."

"I wouldn't dream of it."

Chapter Two

Jenna Peterson's Guide to Dating Emotionally Unavailable Men:

Don't be fooled into believing that emotionally unavailable men don't have deep feelings. They have a lot, in fact, but they don't know how to show it. So get your shovel out and hone those detective skills, because you're going to have to dig deep to find them.

"All heck has broken loose!" I can hear my mom yelling from somewhere outside near the little orange building I've spent the day in and where I'm now tallying up today's sales. It's been a busy day, and I could have used a slower one after last night. Josie got home later than she thought she would, and we ended staying up way later than we should have. But it was worth it. Even though I've had a massive headache all day and my cheeks still ache from laughing so much.

I look through the ticket window that I shut against the cool fall evening just after the pumpkin patch closed and see my mom walking by in that frantic way she does — her back ramrod straight, her feet practically stomping, her hands fisted. An orange beret atop her head.

I open the window. "The word is *hell*, mom," I yell out to her.

This makes her stop in her tracks and she does a full body turn toward me, throwing a scowl in my direction. We could turn this place into a haunted house at night if we get Dana Peterson in the right mood. We would just have everyone say that her pumpkin pie is mediocre and then set her free to terrorize everyone. It would be a lie, though—her pumpkin pie is amazing. It's a family recipe only the sisters are privy to.

She points a finger at me, her drawn-on eyebrows looking extra high today. She's taught me many things, but the cautionary tale about overplucking her brows in the late 90s has been some of her most important work. "Jenna Jo Peterson, I don't want to hear that word out of your mouth."

I'm thirty years old and my mom is still correcting my language. I roll my eyes and go to shut the window I just opened, but I feel like poking the bear a little more. "I learned it from watching HBO," I tell her, and she scowls at me. "What's going on?" I ask, my voice innocent.

Of course, I know what she's in a huff about: Josie out in the field on a tractor ride with none other than the Rogue Pirate, Reece Cavanaugh. A beautiful specimen of a man who happens to have a patch over his left eye. Hence the pirate moniker. It was from some sort of freak accident when he was a child. He's been forbidden to trespass on these lands for over fifteen years now, per the sisters.

I saw it all with my own eyes: Josie in her pumpkin costume, hopping on that tractor and straight into Reece's lap, them riding off into the sunset, with the sisters both doing their best to try and stop it. I've got video to prove it.

"You know very well what's going on," my mom says, putting her hands on her bony hips. She's always been a tiny little thing, both her and my aunt Lottie. My average height and child-bearing hips come from the Peterson side. "Your cousin and that pirate," she goes on. I catch the exaggeration of the word *pirate* in both her tone and the spit that comes flying from her mouth, illuminated by the setting sun behind her. So pretty. "And now your aunt Lottie has run off and no one can find her."

"She's probably making a voodoo doll of Reece up in the attic," I say, throwing the idea out there just to be flippant.

My mom gives me a look that would have sent me running for the cornfields when I was younger. But she doesn't scare me anymore. Well, maybe a little. But I've got a window between us that I can shut and a door I can lock if need be. I'm safe in my little orange cocoon.

"Well, let me know if you see her," she says before turning to walk toward the main house, where Josie grew up. She turns back just as I'm about to shut the window. "I like your hair today," she says.

"Thanks, Mom." I run a hand through my highlighted dark-blond strands. I just had them touched up last week.

"And stand up straight, Jenna. Do you want to develop a hump?"

And there it is. The little slight I knew she'd somehow worm into the conversation. I reach up and touch the ring on my necklace. *Give me strength, Grandma Peterson.*

It's always something with my mom. Sure, she's quick to dole out the compliments. And they're sincere when they come from her. My mom is a lot of things, but patronizing is not one of them. But just as quick as she is to compliment, she's also ready and armed with her critiques. *Jenna, how could you move away to those scary mountains? Jenna, how can you be thirty and still haven't found a good man? Jenna, you should talk to your sister and get some tips on how to settle down.* Ha! Like that would ever happen. *Jenna, can't you get a real grown-up job and stop playing with makeup?* She clearly doesn't know what an aesthetician does since she's never once visited the spa I work at. She's not really a spa kind of woman.

I shut the window in her face with as much exaggeration as I can muster—without breaking the dang thing—and see her shaking her head as she turns and walks toward the main house, which is just a four-minute walk from the house my parents built on the Peterson property. It was kind of like *Full House*, but on a farm. No Uncle Jesse, which is a huge bummer. And the chorus to the opening credit song would have gone something like: *Everywhere you look, everywhere you go, there's a sister all up in your business.*

One of my favorite parts about working here during our busiest season is that everyone has so much going on that no one has time to get up in each other's business. Normally we can fly under the radar during this time. Apparently not this year. Poor Josie.

I close my eyes for a second and take a deep breath. I love my mom, but on days like this, I'm grateful I live in my own place thirty minutes away. Maybe someday I can live a couple of continents away. That still feels too close. Maybe Mars will be habitable at some point.

I get back to working on tallying up the sales, and just as I'm getting into my groove, the door to the office flies open and in walks a slightly breathless and pink-cheeked Josie. Her hair is mussed and her lips are a little on the swollen side, but her smile is so wide I can nearly see her back molars.

She shuts the door, locks it, and leans up against it, her chest moving up and down like she's just run a marathon.

"I ran all the way here," she says.

"From the back field?" I ask, my eyes wide. That's a pretty decent jaunt.

"I couldn't take the risk of being caught by the sisters," she says, trying to catch her breath.

"Well, you just missed my mom; she was headed toward your house."

Josie closes her eyes and takes a large inhale. "Holy shiz," she says.

"Sooooo." I raise one eyebrow and give her an exaggerated smirk. "I take it his tractor's sexy?" I say, referring to the Kenny Chesney song.

"You have no idea." She waves a hand in front of her face and drags her pumpkin-clad self to one of the chairs in the office and plops herself down in it.

"You kissed?" I say, eyes wide.

All she can do is nod. And smile. And keep waving the hand in front of her face.

This is pretty huge. Reece Cavanaugh was the one that got away for Josie. Or rather the pirate that got away. Only, he was never actually captured in the first place. It was just an unrequited crush in high school on Josie's part. He was three grades ahead of us—one grade above Oliver.

Josie's crush was so big that she wrote a story about him. It was called *Reece the Rogue Pirate*, and it was full of adventurous tales that delved into the . . . how shall I say this . . . uh, steamier genre of writing. It was quite advanced for a fifteen-year-old. A lot of "carnal knowledge" as the sisters called it.

Writing has always been a talent of Josie's. When we were young, she'd make up stories for us as we played together. My favorites were when she'd create mysteries about things that were actually lost around the farm. Like the case of the missing rake. She made up this elaborate story about how it was taken by a band of evil barn mice—their leader named Oliver, of course. All the bad guys in her tales were either named Oliver or Olivia.

Oliver really did turn out to be a bad guy in Josie's story, though. No one would have known what she wrote about Reece if it hadn't been for him. He found it, made copies of it, and spread it around school. Josie was forever known as the *Reece the Rogue Pirate* girl after that. And the nickname still exists to this day, fifteen years later, probably because the story made it online somehow and has been read by many people near and far.

The scandal—if you can call it that—caused a lot of angst for Josie, especially in high school, and a lot of problems with the sisters. When a young Josie was asked how she could write such an adult story full of carnal knowledge, she blamed it on a free trial of HBO. And that's why there isn't cable or streaming in either of the sisters' houses to this day.

The sisters, however, were sure that something had actually happened between Reece and Josie. Which was not true. Josie had never even spoken a word to Reece in high school. It didn't matter how many times we swore up and down that nothing was going on between the two of them, the sisters wouldn't believe us.

But now it seems like things might actually be happening between them, as Reece—who's divorced and has a young daughter—has recently been worming his way into Josie's life and they've taken a ride on a tractor. That sounds like a euphemism. But this was an actual tractor ride, apparently with some kissing.

I'm loving all of this. I love that Josie's been happier than I've seen her in a long time, and I'm loving that the return of the pirate has the sisters all tied up in knots. That's a win-win in my book. I'm also grateful that we're no longer hiding from him anymore like we had to when she was trying to avoid running into him. I actually pulled a hamstring jumping behind a banana display at the grocery store so he didn't see us.

"I need details," I say to a starry-eyed Josie.

"Okay," she says, her cheeks pinking even more. "I feel like I'm hopped up on caffeine right now; my hands are even jittery." She holds them out for me to see.

"Here," I say, sliding the heavy donation jar so that it's between us. It's nearly three-quarters full today. The people of Carson City are the best. "Put those hands to use and help me count this up while you spill."

She seems happy to help as we both dig in and start separating bills and she tells me all about what went down between her and Reece on that tractor.

We're giggling like a couple of lovesick teenagers as she's giving me a play-by-play when something catches my eye. It's a fifty-dollar bill with something written on it.

"This is weird," I tell Josie, holding up the money so she can see it.

"What's up?" Josie looks over at me.

"There's a note on this bill." I show Josie. "It looks like it's from someone's grandparents."

Handwritten in blue ink, in meticulous writing along the bottom of the bill, it says, *We love you so much! Save this for a rainy day. Granny and Grandpa. C & J St. Claire.*

"I wonder why someone would donate that?" Jenna says, leaning toward me so she can see it.

"Maybe they didn't mean to?" I reach up and touch the gold band on my necklace. It's a source of comfort for me, and I think I would be lost without it. What if this money is like that for someone else?

"That would be so sad. Or," she says, and I turn my head toward her to see her eyes bright and her eyebrows high up on her forehead—the look she always gives me before she's about to go into storytelling mode. "Maybe it belongs to some hot rich guy who was kidnapped. Of course, the kidnappers would be named Olivia and Oliver."

"Of course," I say.

"A rich man—wait, a rich, *hot* man—"

"And single," I interject.

"Obviously," she says, cocking her head to the side and letting her shoulders fall, giving me the universal body language for *duh*. "And that rich, hot, and *very* single man was taken from his home in the middle of the night because Oliver and Olivia were looking to get a payout."

"It makes perfect sense," I say, giggling.

"The man is being held captive in a cabin in Aspen Lake, and one of the kidnappers—the lazier and uglier one named Oliver—decided to take a break from all the kidnapping and take his bratty kid to Peterson's Pumpkin Patch, where he used the money he stole from Rich Guy's wallet."

"I like it," I say.

"And somehow this fifty-dollar bill is the key to everything. To finding the man, to getting Oliver and Olivia behind bars where they belong. And, of course, there's a reward."

I pull my head back. "You mean like pirate booty? Why does everything have to come back to pirates with you?"

She laughs. "Or it could just be some fifty-dollar bill with writing on it."

"How boring," I say, looking at the money.

"Maybe you should do a little investigating? See if it belongs to someone."

I scrunch my brow. "How would I go about doing that?"

"I don't know." She lifts one pumpkin costume–clad shoulder and drops it. "You have some decent stalker skills. Or there's always the internet." She points to my phone on the desk in front of us.

"I suppose it wouldn't hurt to do a little digging."

"Maybe the kidnapped hot guy will be the man of your dreams."

"I won't hold my breath," I say.

Chapter Three

Jenna Peterson's Guide to Dating Emotionally Unavailable Men:

It's important that you have a lot of patience when dating an emotionally unavailable man. Try channeling the Dalai Lama for help.

"My gosh, are you still at it?" my coworker Chantelle asks as she enters the break room and sees me on my laptop. She left me sitting in the same exact spot over an hour ago.

"Any luck?" She tugs on the bottom of her navy-blue scrub top, the one with the Aspen Lake Lodge Spa logo embroidered in the upper right-hand corner, before she plops herself down in one of the white chairs next to me. She tucks her dark hair behind her ear as she looks at my screen, her flawless ebony skin practically glowing in the overhead lighting.

I blow air out of my mouth, slowly and dramatically. "I've narrowed it down a little more, I think," I tell her.

To say that this whole search for the owner of the fifty-dollar bill has become an obsession is an understatement. It's been only five days, but it's taken over my thoughts during work and at night before I go to sleep in the cute little condo I rent in Aspen Lake. Also, when I'm in the car, on the phone, in the bathroom . . . so, basically all parts of my day. Whenever I have free time, I'm looking on the internet. I needed a distraction, not a new hobby, but here we are: I'm obsessed. I haven't watched even one minute of my favorite Turkish drama. This is saying a lot.

I didn't know where to start, to be honest. Contrary to what Josie said, my stalker skills are lacking. My first step was to literally google "How to find someone with only a last name." I was hoping for a task list or something, but in truth, it was unhelpful. They were mostly answers on how to find a person when you don't know their last name. Which seemed ridiculous. Unless it's an uncommon name, it would be like looking for a needle in a haystack—imagine trying to find a William or an Ashley if that's all you had to go on. A last name should be easier. *Should* being the critical word here. Because it's not so easy, even with the not-often-used last name of St. Claire.

I spent some time looking at old census data since you can't access the new stuff. I made an account on one of those ancestry sites, which only helped a little. I suppose a career in private investigation is not in the cards for me.

"Don't leave me hanging," Chantelle says, pointing at the screen.

"So, there are like over seven hundred St. Claires in the United States."

She pulls her head back. "You're going to try to contact them all?"

"No," I say, shaking my head. "I've been narrowing it down to people that are older and have names that start with C and J."

"And how many did that get you to?"

21

"I've found around thirty."

"So, then what?"

"I'm trying to narrow it even further, but that's proving to be harder."

She purses her lips, her face taking on a contemplative look. "Can I ask you something?"

I've been working with Chantelle for over a year now; we've spent a lot of time together, mostly in this very break room we're sitting in now. I know all about her tumultuous relationship with her boyfriend, Cal, which is short for Calvin, and her love affair with her fawn-colored pug named Miss Piggy. I also know that if I tell her no, she'll ask me anyway.

"Sure," I say.

"Why bother" — she waves a hand around at my computer — "with all this?"

I let out a breath. "I don't know."

"It's only fifty bucks," she says.

"That's true." I reach up and touch my necklace.

"We could buy us some yummy drinks with that." She winks a gorgeous dark-brown eye at me.

"That is also true," I say. "I just . . . at first it was something to do, something to get my mind off stuff."

"What stuff?"

"Like, you know . . . stuff."

"Man stuff?"

"No," I say, and then in the same breath, "okay, yes."

"Ooooh, tell Chantelle your man problems. Is it Mr. Hot Doctor?" It's serious business when Chantelle starts talking about herself in the third person.

"What?" I say, my face scrunched up, giving her a very are-you-freaking-kidding-me glare. "No. No way."

"I mean, he has been checking you out," she says.

"He checks everyone out," I say.

Mr. Hot Doctor, also known as . . . actually, I can never remember his real name. How objectifying of me. It's not my nickname, though; Chantelle came up with it. He's only been here for a month or so, and his last name is something hard to remember. It's something like Shawarma. Nope, that's a yummy Middle Eastern dish. It starts with a *sh* sound, I do know that. Anyway, he comes to the spa a couple of times a week because we do some minor medical treatments here that have to be overseen by a doctor. He's handsome, he's a flirt, he's totally looking for a hookup, and he's absolutely emotionally unavailable. So of course I find him incredibly attractive. Which means I need to stay far, far away.

"Who, then?"

"It's hard to explain," I say.

"I'm listening," she says, giving me a serious face.

"I got invited to Cam's wedding."

"Nooooo," she says, drawing out the word like we're on *Dr. Phil* and they just announced who the baby's father really is. "Wait, who's Cam again?"

I shake my head and look to the ceiling, but do it all with a smile on my face. Typical Chantelle. I've told her about Cam; I know I have. Some days we have a lot of downtime in this break room.

"My last boyfriend?" I say.

She shakes her head, still not sure. We broke up before Chantelle came to work here, but I know I've talked about him. He was my last official boyfriend.

"Tall, blond adventurous type?"

"Oh yeah." She snaps her fingers. "The one with the RBF?"

"No, that was another ex."

My ex, Brian, really did have RBF. Or RWF—resting witch face—as the sisters say, to both pumpkin up the acronym and get rid of the swear. He *did* look like he was constantly scowling. And he never smiled in pictures. Not with teeth, at least. But when he met Gwen, she apparently brought out that gorgeous smile I could only coax out occasionally. This is all according to Instagram of course. I tell myself that right after those pictures were taken, he immediately went back to his regularly scheduled glower.

She snaps her fingers once. "Cam made you jump out of a plane."

"That's the one."

"He's getting married?"

I tap my finger on my nose. "He sure is."

"And you need a distraction? I thought you were okay with the breakup."

"I am," I say. "Or, at least I was. But then, he got engaged. And I don't know . . ."

"Do you wish he was marrying you?"

This makes me pause. Do I wish that announcement were for Cam and me? No. No, I don't. I really did think I loved Cam, even if I'm not totally sure I know what love feels like— certainly not the reciprocated kind. But there was something missing between him and me. I don't know if Cam ever knew me all that well. We spent so much time talking about him, since that's my toxic trait/gift and all—getting people to talk. Rather than being his partner, I kind of felt like I was playing a role in Cam's life movie. A walk-on part of sorts. So, no, I don't wish that.

"No," I say, shaking my head emphatically. "I don't wish it was me."

"So, then what's this all about?" She points to my open browser with the words "C. St. Claire" in the search bar.

"I'm more curious than anything. Like . . ." I stop talking, looking at the ceiling for the right words. "Kind of like I'm drawn to it. Is that dumb?"

"Nope," she says, shaking her head. "You do what you want with your time. But—" She holds up her index finger, much in need of a manicure. One of the pitfalls of working at a spa: all that product can really mess with your hands. "If you give up and want to get drinks instead, you know I'm here for you."

I smile. "You'll be the first person I spend it with." Really it would go back in the jar at the farm. We still have so far to go before we have the money we need for the barn.

"So, explain to me what you're doing," Chantelle says.

I angle the laptop toward her and click on the first search result, which is an obituary I found for a Charles St. Claire from ten years ago.

"I found this one that's a good lead. But he died in Raleigh, North Carolina, and was buried there too," I tell Chantelle. "But the obituary said that his wife's name is Barbara, and on the money it says *C & J*, so I'm assuming this is out."

"Unless Barbara had a nickname that started with a J?" Chantelle throws out, taking on a vibe that's Sherlockesque, like she is now on the case with me.

"See how complicated this is?" I say, feeling deflated.

"What's complicated?" asks Heather as she enters the break room.

"Jenna's mystery fifty-dollar search."

25

"You still working on that?" Heather asks as she opens the small white refrigerator and pulls out a can of Diet Coke; the sound of the tab popping and the fizz of the drink fills the small room.

Heather is another coworker at the spa. While Chantelle and I do mainly facials and body scrubs, Heather is the head massage therapist. When most clients see that tiny five-foot-nothing bombshell of a woman walking toward them, they scoff at the idea that she's worth the hefty price this spa charges for massages. But when they leave here, they almost always come back for more. She may be petite, but she is mighty. I've gotten some bruises from a deep-tissue massage to prove it.

"I'm narrowing it down," I say, giving her the same answer I gave Chantelle. Clearly, they are both judging me. I should have kept it all to myself.

"Let me see a picture of it," Heather says as she takes a seat on the other side of me and leans back in her chair.

I pull out my phone and she looks at it, studying the picture I took of the back of the bill where the writing is. This is the first time she's seen it, since she didn't seem all that interested when I brought it up at the beginning of the week.

Her eyebrows move up her forehead. "St. Claire?"

"Yeah," I say. "Do you know any?"

"Well, there is the St. Claire family that owns the Aspen Lake Boating Company. They've been around here probably for decades."

I look to Chantelle and then back at Heather. "You know them?"

"Well, not all of them, but I think I made out with one of the sons years ago." She looks wistfully at the ceiling.

"You . . . think?" Chantelle asks.

She waves her words away. "I made out with a lot of guys in high school." She gives a little shrug.

Chantelle and I look at each other again. Heather somehow always surprises us. She met her husband right after graduating high school, got married young at nineteen, and got pregnant almost right away. Then another baby two years later. She's only forty and practically an empty nester. She's also churchy in a way that's admirable — always willing to pray for anyone, often quoting a scripture when offering advice, never chastising or being judgy. The woman barely participates in gossip, which can be annoying. She can also seem somewhat naive about the goings-on of the world. Which isn't a bad thing. I sort of find it refreshing. But every now and then she drops a cuss word that would probably make the sisters faint, and now we find out she made out with "a lot of guys" in high school. There's nothing wrong with that, of course — I could have lettered in kissing boys in high school if that were a thing — it just seems . . . not like Heather.

"You made out with a lot of guys in high school?" Chantelle asks, her chin landing on her chest.

I hold up my hand, palm toward Chantelle. I know if I don't stop this train, we will go down the track — because I really, *really* want to. Like, what is "a lot" according to Heather? But if we do, I'll forget to come back to the information she might have. "Let's circle back to that," I say to her. "First, tell me more about the St. Claires."

"What's there to know?" She lifts one shoulder and then takes a drink of her soda. "They've been around here for a long time; the boating company has been passed down through generations, I guess. Growing up, it was always about the St. Claires around here. They're kind of like Aspen Lake royalty."

"I've never even heard of them or the boating company," I say.

"You didn't grow up here," she says. "Aspen Lake is a smaller town than Carson City."

She's not wrong. But even so, running a farm that's well known in the area, the Petersons are also a family that's been around for generations. But we aren't known as royalty — more like the local hillbillies.

"And you've been just sitting on this info?" Chantelle scrunches her nose at Heather.

"I didn't know the specifics," she says.

Chantelle points a finger at me. "You better look it up."

After a quick search, I pull their website up, the Aspen Lake Boating Company logo appearing at the top as the rest of the page starts to populate. I scroll down, looking at pictures of the storefront and the showroom, and then pictures of boats with scenic backgrounds of the lake.

"They sell . . . boats," I say, no inflection in my tone.

"Shocking," Chantelle says sarcastically. "Why don't you look for an 'About Us' page or something?"

I scroll back up to the top, and sure enough, there's a tab with "About Us" on it. I click on it, and it opens up with the words "Our History" and a lengthy detailing of the company's story.

"Aspen Lake Boating Company is the oldest boating company in the area," I start to read from the top of the page. "Tracing back to its beginning in nineteen twenty when its progenitor, Jacob St. Claire, first laid eyes on the beautiful lake. St. Claire knew this would be the place for him. Starting out as a commercial fisherman, he worked until they outlawed — "

"Let me stop you right here," Chantelle says, her eyebrows pulled low so that they almost hood her eyes. She looks at the screen and then back at me. "You don't plan on reading this entire thing to us, do you?"

"Well, I . . ."

"How about you just skim it and give us the details," she says while drumming her fingers on the table.

"I didn't mind it," Heather says.

"All three of us have clients in fifteen minutes," Chantelle reminds us. "From the sound of that history and the speed Jenna was reading it, we might be here for another six hours."

It's true, I had been reading it slowly. But that was because my mind had started racing with thoughts. A thread of hope blossoming inside my chest.

"Right," I tell them. "Hold on."

I read the document quickly, skipping over areas that are about the boating industry as a whole. Both Chantelle and Heather wait patiently as I scan. I have to stop once to ask Chantelle to end her finger drumming since it was distracting me.

"Oh my gosh," I say as I'm about three-quarters down the page. "So the original owner, Jacob, got married and had a son who he named Jacob, and Jacob Jr. took over the company in nineteen sixty, and he married a woman named Carol." I give both Chantelle and Heather wide eyes at this information.

"C. and J. St. Claire," Chantelle says, and Heather claps animatedly.

"Could this be it?" I ask them both, feeling a burst of adrenaline move through me.

"I'd say your chances are high," says Chantelle. "You should call them."

I scan down the document. "Wait," I tell Chantelle as she grabs my phone to make the call. "It says that Jacob Jr. died two years ago and his wife, Carol, a year after that. The business is now run by their grandson, Aidan St. Claire."

"Oh, right—the boy in high school was named Jake," says Heather, her eyes moving up to the ceiling as she recalls, her lips forming into a pucker. "Or it could have been John. I really don't remember."

Chantelle eyes her, warily. She looks to me. "So, ask the grandkid."

"Should I?" Chantelle nods her head yes, while Heather seems to be still contemplating the boy she locked lips with once. "What if it's not him, though?"

"Only one way to find out," says Chantelle, pointing at my phone.

I swallow. I actually didn't have a plan for once I got to this part. I don't know if I even thought I'd get this close. I kind of thought I'd have to do more research or make a bunch of calls before I got this kind of lead.

Chantelle slides my phone over to me. "Do it before we have to get back to work." She points up at the clock on the wall nearest the door. "Clock is ticking."

I let out a breath. "Okay," I say, picking up my phone.

I find the number on the website and type it in and then let my finger hover over the green circle with the white phone icon. I'm feeling lots of butterflies, wondering how this is even going to go. So much so that it's keeping me from pushing the button.

What will I even say? *Hey there, are you missing some money that you might have accidentally donated to help some farmers rebuild their burned-down barn?* Maybe he's never been to the farm and the money had exchanged a few hands before it landed in there. This is feeling too complicated. I need a minute to work it out.

Before I can say this out loud, Chantelle reaches over and presses the call button.

"Chantelle," I exclaim loudly as ringing can be heard through the speaker on my phone.

"We don't have all day," she says, folding her arms as she sits back in her chair.

"Aspen Lake Boating Company," a female voice says through the line.

"Uh, yeah hi . . . I'm . . ." I look to Chantelle and Heather and consider hanging up. I need more time! They both give me nods of encouragement. I lick my lips quickly and then say: "So, I'm uh . . . wondering if I can speak with Aidan St. Claire?"

"Can I tell him what this is regarding?"

"Um . . . well, it's kind of hard to explain," I say. I make a face at Chantelle and Heather like, *What am I doing?* Heather gestures with her hand for me to keep going. "I might have something he wants."

Oh gosh, that could be taken so many ways. Threatening? Sexual? Chantelle and Heather both look at me like I have two heads. I swallow, getting ready to restate my purpose. But before I do, the receptionist says, "Let me put you through."

I'd half expected her to put me off, telling me she'll take a message or to call back at a different time, but apparently she didn't really care what I was calling for.

After a handful of seconds of hold music and one incident where I tried to hang up but both Chantelle and Heather stopped me, there's a clicking noise on the other end, and then a gruff voice says, "This is Aidan St. Claire."

Chapter Four

Jenna Peterson's Guide to Dating Emotionally Unavailable Men:

Saying thank you is hard for a man if he's not in touch with his feelings. Don't take it personally even if you really, really, really want to.

"Mr. St. Claire?" I say into the speaker of my phone.

"Yes," he says. There's no inflection in his voice. No upward turn of the word. Just a hard *yes*.

"Hi, I'm Jenna." I touch the ring on the chain around my neck and then look to both Chantelle and Heather for reassurance. I kind of wish that Chantelle would grab the phone out of my hand and just finish this for me. That feels like something she would do. But she doesn't. She just looks at me, bobbing her head with her eyes wide—nonverbally telling me to say something. But words aren't coming. I feel like my tongue is swelling in my mouth. This whole thing is so awkward, and I don't like awkward. Also, I feel stupid. Now that I'm talking to a real-life person on the other end of the line, I'm starting to wonder why I was so caught up in this whole thing. I'm feeling like I should have left the money in the jar and just written it off as no big deal.

"Can I help you?" he asks, his tone this time sounding irritated.

"Uh, yes," I start. "So, this is kind of strange, but I work for Peterson's Pumpkin Patch. On the weekends, not during the week. During the week I work at Aspen Lake Lodge Spa." Oh my gosh, I'm babbling.

"Just tell him," Chantelle says in a loud whisper, nudging me with a hand on my arm.

"Okay," Aidan St. Claire says on the other end, his tone sounding skeptical.

"Anyway, last weekend I found some, uh, money in our donation jar. And it had some words written on it that led me to believe it might have been put there by mistake and that it might belong to you, or maybe someone related to you."

I'm nervous. I have the cold sweats, where every other part of my body feels chilled and goose pimply but my pits are sweaty like I've just run a marathon. This is all so stupid. The whole thing. Finding the money, thinking there's something behind it. Wasting nearly a week searching, and now actually calling someone? I'm a total idiot. I should have taken up overeating cupcakes or embroidery for a distraction. Not this. One thing is for sure: if this call doesn't lead to anything, I'm done looking.

I can hear some shuffling sounds through the phone, followed by a couple of cuss words and then a clearing of the throat, and then silence.

"Mr. St. Claire?" I ask, wondering if maybe the line was disconnected.

"Is it fifty dollars?"

My brows move up my forehead, my eyes wide as I look at Chantelle and Heather, who are both giving me the same face.

"Yeah—yes. That's correct," I say.

He exhales loudly. "Does it say from Granny and Grandpa? C. and J. St. Claire?"

"Yes, that's it," I say, my voice sounding slightly excited now, as I'm feeling not quite as stupid as I did just a minute ago. I look from Chantelle to Heather and then back to Chantelle again. This time we all have big smiles on our faces.

"I'd like it back," he says. "I can give you replacement money."

Aha! I was right. The money is important to him.

"Uh, yeah, okay," I say. I'd tell him not to worry about it, but we still need money for the barn, so I'm not going to say no to that.

"How did you find me?" he asks, his tone still gruff. His voice has been hard and edgy this entire conversation. I don't know what I expected. I don't think I'd gotten to this part of my imagining. I guess I'd expected that once I found the owner, they might tell me that they didn't actually need the money, that they intended it for the jar, and then maybe I'd get a thank-you for reaching out. Or that it would be someone who accidentally donated the money and would be beyond thrilled that I contacted them. Like so grateful, they might reward me with even more money I could donate to the barn.

But I didn't expect little to no warmth from the person. I guess I shouldn't fault him. I'd already declared to myself how ridiculous this whole thing was. Regardless, the owner of the money has been found. I can go back to my regularly scheduled life of . . . well, something. Maybe I really will learn embroidery.

"I just did a little searching online and took a chance," I tell him. I'm not about to say I spent the last five days letting this whole thing take over my brain. My *life*, actually.

"Well . . . okay," he says, pausing between the two words as if he's struggling to find the right ones to say.

"How should I get it to you?"

"I can come to you," he says. "Where did you say you work?"

"I'm at the spa at the Aspen Lake Lodge."

"I can be there by five," he says.

"Sounds good," I say, and then after awkward goodbyes where I said it not once, not twice, but three times— *whyyyyyyy*—we hang up.

"Well, I guess that mystery is solved," Chantelle says, standing up from her chair and stretching her back.

I look at my phone. "I guess it is." Now that it's over, it all feels sort of anticlimactic. Like a super boring ending to a movie or book. I'm not sure what I was expecting, but that wasn't it. At least the mystery of the money has been solved, and at least my distraction had a purpose, I guess.

I'm standing at the front counter of the spa at exactly five o'clock waiting for Aidan St. Claire to arrive. I've tripled-checked that the money is in the pocket of my white work scrubs so I can hand it to him when he gets here.

"Hot date?" asks Missy, who works in reception greeting clients, taking payments, and scheduling appointments. Her bright-blond hair is swept into a ponytail, and she's wearing lavender-colored scrubs.

The spa feels very fitting for Aspen Lake, with the beadboard natural wood paneling on the walls and the grand half-circle knotty pine desk that serves as our check-in counter, the place where Missy spends most of her time. It's got a cabin-like feeling to it, with a gas fireplace and high-backed upholstered chairs in the front reception space as well as the waiting area. My favorite part is the indoor waterfall with the rock backdrop at the end of the hall where all our service rooms are located. It's relaxing to work here. Not quite as relaxing as being a client, though.

"Oh sure," I say, gesturing to what I'm wearing with a downward swoop of my hand. "I'm sure to knock his socks off in this ensemble."

"White scrubs are my favorite," Mr. Hot Doctor says as he waltzes into the reception area, clearly having heard what I just said. He winks at me, and I shake my head, smiling while I do. He's a schmoozer, that one. And so many red flags. So many that his red flags have red flags. He's the kind of guy that looks well put together on the outside, like his grooming habits, and probably his giant house (that he likes to talk about) overlooking Aspen Lake, at first glance, would look meticulous. But under his bed and in his closet? Complete disaster. We're talking multiple junk drawers here.

In my experience, there are many types of emotional unavailability. Each one of the last four guys had different qualities that initially attracted me to them. Brian was a real alpha male. A hot jerk. He was cool in his aloofness, and I found that intriguing. He sort of swept me off my feet at first. Not by anything he said or did, necessarily, but just by being him. I'd only read about guys like him—meeting Brian was the first time I realized those kinds of men really existed.

Garrett, well, he was a different sort of emotionally stunted guy. He considered himself a poet, and the poems would come to him in strange places, like a nightclub. Many a sonnet was written on the back of a cocktail napkin. We hit it off one night, and the relationship moved at lightning speed. I found it exciting and different. Until I figured out that this was just a thing he did in every relationship.

Cam was so much fun. Always looking for a distraction, something adventurous for us to do. He was also so hot and cold all the time. Telling me he wanted to be with me forever one day, and then acting like we weren't even a thing the next. No wonder Josie disliked him so much.

Like Mr. Hot Doctor, Matthew used excessive flirting to cover up his feelings. And it was fun at first. But then I soon realized I wasn't the only one he was flirting with. It was an everyone kind of thing. He'd even flirt with all the female servers while we were out to dinner. Which was usually uncomfortable for the server *and* for me. Unless they flirted back, which was actually the case sometimes. Then it was just painful for me.

"So, what are you waiting here for?" Mr. Hot Doctor asks, leaning on the counter near me, his chin resting in his hands, his blue eyes doing a sort of sparkling thing, looking like he's going to hang on every word that comes out of my mouth. Dang, he's *good*.

If I were going to flirt back, I'd say something coy like, *That's none of your business.* But because I'm swearing off men like Mr. Hot Doctor, I simply say, "Just waiting on a friend so I can return something." I don't say *stranger* or give a clue to what I'm returning because that would only open the door to questions, which would then lead to more flirting.

"Well, good luck with all that," he says before giving me a slick-looking smile as he turns and leaves the reception area. He gives Missy a little nod as he walks away, and I watch as her eyes follow him out. I don't blame her; he's quite good looking with his well-styled dark-blond hair and that perfectly trimmed beard. He gives off big Chris Evans vibes. Or maybe it's Chris Pine. I can never keep all the famous Chrises straight.

Just in case Mr. Hot Doctor tries to make a reappearance, and feeling a bit like a stalker as I'm now fully staring out the small window cutout on the front door, I walk the few steps from the front counter, open the door, and go outside to wait. The mountain air is chilly this late-September evening, but it feels good to breathe it in.

I feel for the money in my pocket again, just in case it grew legs and ran off or I was pickpocketed by Mr. Hot Doctor. I wouldn't put it past him. The money is still there, thank goodness.

It will be weird to have nothing to research tonight. Five days of this and it's practically become a habit. Which is funny because I've been working out regularly for the past six years and I still feel like it's something I have to force myself to do. Twenty-one days to make a habit is a joke.

After a few minutes, the coldness is beginning to move from refreshing to bordering on bone chilling. I've decided to go back inside when I see a fairly tall man walking toward me in a black leather jacket, a gray scarf dangling from his neck.

He looks up at the sign on the building and then at me.

"Mr. St. Claire?" I ask the man.

"That's me," he says, in that same gruff tone he used over the phone. I've found people can have different personas on the phone than in person. Clearly Aidan St. Claire only knows how to be gruff and unapproachable. He definitely gives off those vibes.

He looks like his voice too. Dark, perfectly coiffed hair, ice-blue eyes surrounded by thick, dark eyelashes. I wonder what those eyelashes would do with a little mascara. Which is an odd thought to be having right now. He's got the beginnings of a little scruff around the base of his jaw. He's not exactly what I was picturing when we spoke on the phone. But somehow it all fits. He looks like an upper-class cranky-pants kind of man with a gruff voice. I bet he's the kind of guy who has a place for everything. Nothing askew, everything organized. The kind of guy that lives by his calendar. The apps on his phone are probably posted in alphabetical order or something.

"Well, here you go," I say as I reach into my pocket and pull out the money. I briefly wonder if I should check his ID or something. But this is only fifty dollars, and someone would have to have gone to a lot of work to know that I'd be standing here with it on my person.

I hand it to him, and he takes it with an outstretched hand. He's got nice hands. Large and masculine. I notice he's missing a wedding band on his ring finger, which is neither here nor there. That one is a real habit of mine — looking for rings. Being single in a smallish town for too long will do that to anyone.

He swiftly puts the money in the pocket of the dark-blue jeans he's wearing. "I . . . ," he starts.

"Yeah?"

"Well." He stops himself with a purposeful clearing of his throat. He then reaches up and scratches his jaw. "I appreciate you tracking me down."

"No problem," I say. "I figured it was probably important."

He touches the pocket where the cash is safely tucked away and looks down at the ground with a hard swallow as if he had to force himself to do it. "It is," he says.

"Okay, well then I'm glad you have it, and I'm just going to go back in . . . there." I point over my shoulder at the spa door behind me.

"Sure," he says. "No problem."

I swing the door open thinking about how weird that all was. And also the fact that he didn't once thank me for returning the money to him. He did say he appreciated my effort. So I guess that's a thank-you of sorts. It's in the same family at least.

"Wait," I hear just as I take my first step back inside, my body anticipating the warmth of the spa to help thaw out the cold in my bones. Instead, I turn back toward Aidan St. Claire.

"Yes?"

He reaches into his other pocket — the one that doesn't hold the fifty I just gave him — and pulls out his wallet. "I wanted to give you money to, uh, replace it."

I take in a breath. "Oh, right," I say, letting the door to the spa shut, tucking the warmth back inside.

As he opens his wallet and looks in the bill fold, I have a gnawing feeling I should just let him keep his money niggling at the back of my brain. But I know we need it for the barn. We probably won't raise enough money as it is. Clearly, he's not hurting for cash, if the designer shoes he's wearing are any indication.

"Thank you," I say, demonstrating how easy it is to say those two words. Because it really is that easy.

Aidan hands me a few bills — two twenties and a ten. Now, I know I was just considering telling him to keep his money, but

I'm suddenly struck with a slight irritation. I did go to all the trouble of finding him and giving him back something that seems to be important to him. He couldn't be bothered to give me an extra fiver? For a tip? At the very least?

I put the money in my pocket and then give him a little nod. It's a nod of finality. A goodbye dip of my chin. No more words need to pass between us.

"Can I—" he stops himself again with a clearing of his throat. It's a strange tic, but we've all got them. Mine is sniffling for no reason, which I do right now. Because, why not. But also, my nose is starting to run from the cold. "Can I buy you a drink? You know, for . . . this." He pats the front pocket of his jeans.

"Uh . . . ," I say, trying to work out my apologies because that's going to be an absolute no from me. A definite pass.

"Right there at the Eagle's Den?" He points to the building two doors down from the lodge. A bar that Chantelle, Heather, and I sometimes visit after work. Even if the name annoys me. Eagles have nests, not dens.

"It's fine," I say, shaking my head, imagining sitting at the bar with this stranger of a man. It doesn't sound all that fun. "Don't worry about it."

"I'd really like to," he says. "Please." His brows have moved up his head, and the corners of his lips have turned upward ever so slightly. He looks . . . well, he looks sort of pathetic, honestly. Like saying please was difficult for him. A real trial.

"Um," I say, still trying to think of the right words. I could just say a firm *No, thank you,* and then walk back into the spa. But I don't know, maybe the chill has gotten to my brain because I hear myself say, "Yeah, sure. Sounds good."

What's wrong with me?

Chapter Five

Jenna Peterson's Guide to Dating Emotionally Unavailable Men:

In the beginning of the relationship, you'll find that you have to do most of the talking until they feel comfortable opening up. So bring a lozenge.

Aidan walks toward the Eagle's Den, and I roll my eyes at myself as I follow him up the slight incline to the bar. The sun is just starting to set behind the mountain that downtown Aspen Lake was built on. It's stunning this time of day. Or really any time of day.

I'm mentally kicking myself for saying yes as we walk. *Why?* I regretted it instantly. I sometimes wish I could push a back arrow on my life, or an undo button. Give myself a chance for a redo.

We approach the weathered-on-purpose wooden door of the bar, and Aidan opens it, ushering me in first. Inside, the dimly lit space assaults my nose with a distinct smell of malt and hops, but my body is instantly thankful for the warmer temps as the door shuts behind us.

It's pretty empty—just a couple of guys playing pool over in the corner, and Ed, the bartender, drying a glass behind the bar. Multicolored Christmas lights hang around the place no matter the time of year. A song by the Eagles (fitting, at least) plays on the old jukebox in the corner. I'm pretty sure if you looked up *bar* in the dictionary, this is the picture that would come up. Not all that original. Still, there's a comforting feeling here. Like when you come here you know what you're in for.

"I'll take a stout; whatever you recommend," Aidan says to the bartender when he approaches us, and then gestures with a hand toward me for my order.

"I'll" — I look at Ed, who I know recognizes me, evidenced by the little smirk on his face — "take a Coke."

I feel Aidan's eyes on my profile. "Just a Coke?"

"I don't drink all that much," I say with a quick lift of my shoulders. The truth is drinking was pretty much prohibited by the sisters. Which should have made me want to drink all the more. And I did, mostly in college. But then I realized I don't really like alcohol all that much, except for the odd glass of wine now and then. I usually enjoy doing things that would annoy my mom and aunt, like sexy dancing to "Monster Mash" when it plays over the loudspeakers at the farm or cutting up my orange work shirt so it hangs off my shoulder and shows a little cleavage — they really hated that one. But alcohol just never did it for me.

Aidan gives a quick nod, and the bartender moves down the counter to grab our drinks. We both take seats at the bar, Aidan taking off his jacket and scarf and hanging them over the back of the tall bar chair before he sits.

He leans his forearms on the counter, weaving his fingers together and resting his hands on the wood surface. I fold my arms in front of me and roll my lips together, doing my best to find a place for my eyes to focus on. It's not easy. They keep moving back to Aidan's forearms. He's wearing a light-blue button-down shirt with the sleeves rolled up, and I can't help but notice how defined and sinewy the lower parts of his arms look.

"So," I finally say, forcing my eyes to move over to the lit-up red-and-white Budweiser sign hanging on the wall behind the bar.

"So," he echoes.

Yep, this is going exactly how I thought it would. I sniffle for no reason, and he clears his throat. *Fantastic.*

"How long have you lived in Aspen Lake?" I finally ask him after Ed has dropped off our drinks and Aidan handed him a credit card to pay for them.

"Most of my life," he says.

"Where did you go when you weren't living here?"

"College."

"And where was that?"

"USC."

"Ah, a Trojan." I give him a nod, feeling slightly self-important for knowing the mascot of the Southern California school. My sister Olivia's husband — Reginald the Pretentious, as Josie and I like to call him — went there. I won't ask Aidan if he knows my brother-in-law because that would probably be a point in the wrong column for me if we were keeping score.

He nods back at me, the corners of his lips pulling upward a bit. I'm assuming this is Aidan St. Claire's attempt at a smile. He definitely doesn't dole them out.

"What about you?" he asks with a slight tilt of his head in my direction.

Well, looky here. Are we communicating? Like actual back-and-forth questions? Not that I'm feeling any more

45

comfortable, and by the way Aidan clears his throat every now and then, I'm guessing he's not either. His voice still carries that same note of gruff with a side of aloofness, but actual conversing is happening. I feel like this is a big deal. Like I should text it to Josie. But she doesn't even know that I figured out the fifty-dollar-bill mystery yet.

"University of Nevada, Reno," I answer. It sounds so boring when I say it. But it was actually really fun. Josie and I both went there, and it was only thirty minutes from home, so it still felt like independence but was close enough that we could easily come home on the weekends and help during pumpkin season. Or make the sisters cook real food for us.

I studied communications with an emphasis in public relations and quickly learned that I hated it. I didn't want to spin stories for some corporation—I wanted to hear real stories. While I was there, I worked the front counter at a spa, and it just seemed so much more my style. Being around people one-on-one. My gift—or possibly toxic trait—was made for that. There was so little stress, too, like nothing to take home with you after work. Every day is new and different. So I got my bachelor's and then went to aesthetician school in Reno. Much to my mother's disappointment.

"Sorry, I don't think I know the mascot."

"Wolf Pack," I say. I can't fault him for not knowing. No one does.

Silence moves over us again, except for the sound of pool balls cracking, a country song I don't recognize on the jukebox, and some running water behind the bar. I feel my gut sink because as far as conversations go, that was a bust. Good thing I didn't text Josie. We're now just sitting here, both of us taking intermittent sips of our drinks. Would it be rude for me to guzzle mine, slam the cup on the bar, and then tell him thanks and head back to the spa? Probably. I sometimes hate that Dana Peterson taught me manners.

"So, the money," I say, giving him a little smile. Clearly, I've not given up on this conversation quite yet. "What's that all about?"

Aidan sets his beer down on the bar, keeping his line of sight away from me and toward the wall behind the counter. He's got a very attractive profile. Strong jaw, nice nose. And yep, my eyes just went down to those forearms again. *Nope. Noooooope. Keep your eyes upward, Jenna.*

But upward isn't much better. The man is attractive, okay? From the front, the side, even the backside—yes, I noticed that too, ugh—he's 100 percent hotness. I've been trying not to admit this to myself because I don't want Aidan St. Claire to be attractive. I want him to be, well . . . *not* attractive, and definitely not the type of man that I consider pretty. But he is. He very much is.

Also attractive to me? His closed-off nature and the fact that he's not good at expressing himself—like how he can't answer the simple question I just asked him—and that his conversation skills are lacking. All telltale signs of emotional unavailability. I'd gotten those vibes even on the phone earlier today. I can feel myself wanting to ply him with questions, to peel back who he is layer by layer. It's my special gift/toxic trait that I'm trying to remove from my person. Flies on rotting fruit, remember? I must stop the cycle.

"You don't have to tell me if you don't want to," I say, shutting it down by giving him an out.

He shakes his head. "Sorry, it's not that. I just . . . it's kind of a long story."

Ding, ding, ding. We have a winner! If I had a dime for every time I've heard that reasoning, I'd be a rich woman. "It's kind of a long story" is the easy way of saying "I don't feel like telling you." *I'll take emotional unavailability for five hundred, Alex.*

Oh my gosh, is this irony? Maybe not. I've never known how to define that word. Probably more like coincidental. I wanted something to distract me from the emotionally unavailable men in my past and the fact that they are all married—or getting married—just not to me. So the universe finds me a fifty-dollar bill which leads me to . . . another emotionally unavailable man. Josie is going to laugh so hard when I tell her this. And then probably hug me. Because that's Josie. First, though, I'd have to peel her lips off that pirate. I haven't talked to her in days because she's always with him. I don't mind, I'm so happy for her. I just miss her.

"Okay," I say, and we sit there in silence once again. It's better this way. I'm not going to keep asking him questions like I usually do, looking for a door I can open that will get him to talk. I'll just drink my Coke and leave. Besides, silence is fine. Good, even. I can totally do silence.

"How long have you worked for your family's business?" I ask after what felt like an eternity had passed, though it was probably not even a minute.

I lied. I actually can't do silence. I'm terrible at it. It makes me feel twitchy. Plus, I'm tired of staring at that Budweiser sign. It's imprinting on my brain. I can see it on every surface now, every time I blink.

I'm going with easy questions, the safe kind. But even this question seems to be hard for Aidan to answer, if the quizzical look he's giving me is any indication.

"How do you know that?" he finally asks.

"Oh," I say, shaking my head quickly, closing my eyes briefly. "I read it on the website for your company, under the company history. That's how I worked out that the money might belong to someone there."

Understanding dawns — *no, I'm not a stalker* — and he gives me a slow nod. "I've worked there since I was fourteen."

"Wow," I say, even though I have him beat. I've worked at the pumpkin patch since I could carry a pumpkin. Which was around three. Child labor laws are ignored on a family farm. "And you run the company now?"

Keep it simple, Jenna. Keep. It. Simple.

"That's right," he says.

"What do you do there?"

He reaches up and scratches his neck. "I manage, mostly."

"Sales?"

He shakes his head. "No, I'm not part of that. I leave that to others."

"Not a salesman, then," I say, and Aidan shakes his head. Not that I couldn't have guessed that from the minute I heard him answer the phone. No one wants to buy something from someone who gives off real curmudgeon vibes.

"And it was your great-grandfather that started the company?" I already know the answer to this — I saw it on the website. But I'm keeping it light here, just going through the motions. No big deal.

"That's right," Aidan says, and the gruffness in his tone sounds a little lighter for some reason, sort of like the rough edges of his voice have rounded a tiny bit. There's something there. A little pride maybe?

"That's great," I say. We're silent again. It's a good thing I'm turning over a new leaf here, because Aidan St. Claire would be a hard one to crack. Talking to him feels akin to trying to get water from a cactus.

"I take it you were close to your grandparents?" I say after a bit of uncomfortable silence. This question delves a little deeper than what I'm trying to do here, but it's still safe. Plus, I honestly want to know the story about the money. I find it interesting. I could see if he's open to telling me that much?

"Very," Aidan says.

So many short answers. *Gahhhhhhh*, this is the most torturous drink of all time. I stare at my cup; it's half-full. I could guzzle it now and be back at the spa in a matter of minutes. That sounds so lovely.

Instead, I swallow and try another tactic. "I saw that they passed away not long ago—it was on the website. I'm sorry for your loss." I give him what I hope is an empathetic smile. "I lost my grandparents on my dad's side when I was twelve. I still miss them."

I can still picture those kind, wrinkled faces in my mind. Grandma Peterson—whose wedding band I wear around my neck—was diagnosed with colon cancer and gone within a year, and Grandpa died not long after from what they call *broken heart syndrome*. He was so lost without her. We all were. They both were important to me, but there was just an extra special connection with my grandma.

It was a big loss for us, and even for the community, when they passed away. They were the heart of the farm. My parents and aunt and uncle had big shoes to fill. There are a lot of traditions started by my grandparents that we continue to this day. And some extra obnoxious ones the sisters added later. I sometimes picture Grandpa and Grandma Peterson looking down on us, shaking their heads at some of the craziness.

PUMPKIN SPICE AND NOT SO NICE

Aidan bobs his head up and down, slowly pushing his half-full glass back and forth on the bar, the golden liquid sloshing up each side as he slides it. "It was definitely hard."

"I bet," I say.

It's quiet again. I'm just about to thank him for the drink and head out, but I see Aidan take a couple of breaths as if to start talking. Then he finally says, "I grew up with them, actually. My parents . . . they, uh, divorced when I was ten."

OMG a sentence. Why do I feel like I just won something?

"Wow. Was that a hard age to understand all that?" I ask, inwardly chastising myself for asking him a deeper question. I couldn't help myself. Stupid communication skills.

He dips his chin once. "It was. It was really hard."

I'm thinking that's the end of that, but then he does something unexpected. Aidan turns his body so it's angled more toward mine. His crystal-blue eyes look at me. "My dad — he basically left us and moved to Sacramento. And we — my mom, and me, and my . . . uh, older brother, Jake — had to move in with my grandparents. They helped raise us. Gave us everything we needed."

So it *was* Aidan's brother that Heather made out with. I can't wait to tell her and Chantelle.

"That's so great," I say, trying not to smile at the fact that Aidan has just delivered an entire paragraph's worth of speaking. *Hot damn, Jenna. You've still got it.* "Is that why the money — the fifty dollars — was so important to you?"

Aidan takes a big breath, then a drink of his beer, and then takes another breath. I'm assuming he's going to give me the old "it's a long story" thing again, and then my little bubble of self-congratulations will pop before my eyes.

Instead, he turns even farther in his seat, and I've turned in mine so that now we are face-to-face. "Yeah," he says. "My grandma gave me that fifty-dollar bill when I graduated from high school. It was meant for a rainy day, or for an emergency, or something." He reaches up and scratches the side of his jaw, looking to the side toward the bar. "So, I've had it in my wallet for just over fifteen years now." He looks back at me again. "Until it ended up in that donation jar."

"How did the money get there?"

Chapter Six

Jenna Peterson's Guide to Dating Emotionally Unavailable Men:

Looking for flaws is one of their specialties.

Aidan looks down at his hands; his fingers are intertwined in his lap, his thumbs twiddling. "I was visiting the pumpkin farm with a woman I was dating," he says.

My brain totally caught that *was,* and it lights the word up in my head like it's on a marquee board with big, round globe lights surrounding it. Was! Was! WAS! *Stand down, brain.*

"She wanted to put some money in the donation jar, so I handed her my wallet while I was buying tickets to get in. From . . . I guess, you, maybe?"

I shrug. "Possibly," I say. Selling entrance tickets is my main job on the weekend, but I've been known to ask some of the locals we hire to work the desk so I can help with the cider now and then. It's across from Josie and the room where she reads stories about Priscilla Pumpkin. Or I sometimes wander around chatting with people and doing my best to avoid the sisters.

"I didn't expect her to find that fifty," he continues. "It was tucked in another pocket of my wallet. But somehow, she did."

"And the rest is history," I say, lifting the corner of my mouth in a half smile.

"Yep," he says, mirroring my grin. I think there may have been a hint of a dimple on his right cheek. *Uuuuugh. Have mercy.*

"The donation jar is for the barn, by the way," I say while tamping down my brain—and my hormones. Both had taken off like a speeding train. "It burned down last year. So we appreciate the donation."

He dips his chin just once.

"So you've had the money in your wallet, all this time?"

Both corners of his lips pull upward, and there is most definitely a dimple on that right cheek. *Blargh.* "Yeah," he says. "I've carried it with me since they gave it to me. It's—" he stops himself as if he's looking for the right words. "It's kind of a lucky charm thing." He looks down at his hands again, as if the admission embarrasses him.

"A good-luck charm?" I smile. I may not know Aidan at all, but from what I do know, that little tidbit about him seems out of character, and it surprises me. I'm not usually surprised by people, so I find this intriguing.

He reaches up and scratches his chin. "Yeah, it's kind of foolish."

"I don't think so," I say, shaking my head. "I like that kind of stuff. I got this ring from my grandma." I reach up and tap the gold band hanging around my neck.

His eyebrows move up his forehead. "Oh, I thought maybe that was a wedding ring."

"It is, but it's not mine. I'm . . . not married. I'm kind of done with all that. Relationships and stuff." Why am I telling him this? *Shut up!* "Anyway," I say, dragging out the word.

"It's why I felt like I should try to track you down. Because I have something important from someone I love too."

"Well, that makes me feel better," he says. "Having that money in my wallet . . . it's like they're still with me in a way." He says this to the wall behind the bar, the words breathily falling out of his mouth as if he didn't mean to say them. I'm validated in my thoughts when he shakes his head rapidly, like he's trying to shake himself back into reality.

"I totally get it," I add, trying to ease his discomfort. "It's hard to lose someone you love."

"It is." He nods. He sits there for a minute, pondering. "It sort of feels like something's missing in my life, you know?"

"I do," I say. "It's like you're still you, but not who you used to be."

"Right, that's how it feels," he says, a look of wonderment on his face with his brows up and his mouth slightly open, as if my words have made him feel understood.

"It seems like they were more like parents, rather than grandparents."

He lets out a breath. "They were," he says, his eyes moving to someplace on the floor. "My dad has never really been there, and my mom . . . well, she's had a tough life. So my grandparents were there for all the big things in my life."

"Like what?"

He lifts a shoulder. "Awards ceremonies, graduations. Stuff like that."

"Right," I say. "The important stuff."

We sit in silence for a few beats. Then Aidan looks at me, the left corner of his mouth inching up ever so slightly, and says, "You're easy to talk to."

I give him a smile that was probably more of a wince than a grin. *Crap*. That's not the first time I've heard those words. In fact, I've heard them many, many times. I need to shut this down. I'm unintentionally peeling back layers. I can't help myself. This toxic trait of mine is going to be hard to stop. At least when it comes to members of the opposite sex who have problems expressing themselves and somehow keep popping into my life.

"Yeah," I say on an exhale. "I've been told that before. That's kind of my thing."

Aidan's eyes widen slightly. "Your thing?"

I shrug one shoulder. "People tend to open up to me sometimes."

"Why?"

"Probably because I ask a lot of questions. I'm inquisitive like that."

He scrutinizes my face for a few beats longer than is comfortable. Like he's trying to solve a puzzle. "It's more than that, though," he finally says.

"I honestly don't know," I say. I do know, actually. It's a curse.

"I'm not good at talking to people," he says.

I just smile at him, the word *duh* hanging on the tip of my tongue.

"I've never been any good at it." His shoulders drop slightly, a look of frustration passing over his handsome features. It was quick, but I caught it.

"Well, if you need someone to help you with that, I'm your gal," I say without too much thought. Bonus for Aidan, he'd probably get a marriage out of it. Not with me, of course.

His eyebrows move up his head.

56

"I'm . . . kidding," I say when I realize how that all sounded. "I'm not really your . . . gal."

Why do I keep talking? *Okaaaaay*, it's time to wrap this up. I sniffle for no reason, grab my Coke and take a big gulp, and set it back on the counter with finality. A very distinct I'm-finished-here clunking sound.

"Well, I better go," I say, standing up and scooting back my tall bar chair with my butt.

Aidan takes a breath, seeming sort of taken aback by my abrupt departure. "Sure," he says.

"It was nice to meet you. Thank you for the drink. Maybe I'll see you around the pumpkin patch." I stand up from my seat, ready to get out of here.

His eyebrows pinch together. "Probably not," he says.

"Oh, okay." That was a strange thing for him to say. I know I should leave, but something about that declaration has me curious. What exactly does he mean? "You don't like pumpkin patches?" I ask.

"Uh . . . no, I don't mind them. It was more that particular farm."

Well, he has my attention now. I'm suddenly all ears. "What's wrong with it?" I ask him.

"The family that runs it — the Petersons? They're a strange bunch."

This makes me cock my head to the side as I study Aidan's face. Does he not know what my last name is?

"The Petersons are weird?" I ask, feeling affronted. I mean, we absolutely are. I can say that — and I have many, *many* times — but no one else is allowed to. Certainly not an outsider who's spent only a couple of hours around us.

"I don't mean to offend," he says, probably in response to the stare down I'm currently giving him. "I know you work there."

Work there? Like since I was born? He really doesn't know my last name. Did I never tell him? I sit back down in the seat I'd just vacated.

"What's so weird about them?" I ask him, out of morbid curiosity.

"It's . . . I mean, it's not a big deal." He waves the words away with his hands.

I'm invested now. I need to know what he thinks. I've never had this view before. No one has ever said anything like this to me. Why would they when they know I'm a Peterson? Aidan clearly doesn't.

"No, I really want to know," I say.

He looks at me and then at a spot on the bar. "Where do I begin," he says. "The women that I think run the place? They are so loud. Like, obnoxiously so. And seemed to be on some sort of mission, something about a . . . pirate? Is that some sort of character thing?"

Oh gosh. That's right. That was the day I found that fifty-dollar bill — when Reece whisked Josie off on that tractor. In our defense, that wasn't a normal day at the farm.

"Uh, no," I say awkwardly. "That was just a onetime thing." I'm not about to explain that whole story. It would only add to his assessment.

"And everyone kept using that word — what was it?" He reaches up and scratches his head and then looks to me as if I can fill in the blank for him. But then he points a finger at me, like he's figured it out. "Pumpkiny," he says.

"Pumpkiny? That word bothers you?"

"It's not a word," he says.

I'm annoyed now. I mean, when he puts it that way, it does sound odd. But he's not seeing the true beauty of the farm. What about the hayrides? Or the cider? Or the corn maze? Or my dad and my uncle in their overalls, looking like the quintessential farmers? And to be honest, I think *pumpkiny* is a cute word—even if it's not a real one. Except when Josie's suck-up brother, Oliver, says it. Then it's annoying.

"I was practically accosted by a woman in a pumpkin costume," he continues. "She nearly ran me over."

"I'm sure she didn't mean to," I say, knowing full well that Josie would be mortified if she heard this. She was probably trying to run interference between our mothers and Reece.

"And then, every once in a while, all the employees yell *pumpkin* as loud as they can."

We do do that, but only at the top of every hour. It's . . . tradition. We Petersons have many traditions. I'm not even sure where many of them started.

"And the hats everyone wears, the berets?"

Okay, I'll give him that one.

"It's not very well run," he says. "They could change a lot of things and it would be so much better."

I know I shouldn't ask this next question, but the words fall out of my mouth anyway. "How so?"

"Maybe new management? I'd definitely get rid of the two obnoxious women who look to be running the show."

Get rid of the sisters? But they're the life behind the farm. They may have married into it, but they've taken on the task like they've been a part of it since birth. Along with my uncle and dad, their entire lives have revolved around that farm.

"Their last names are Peterson—the name of the farm?"

He lifts one shoulder. "Maybe they could let someone else run it?"

Is he for real? Yeah, I think I've heard enough.

I look at Aidan, square in the face, ready to hit him straight on with my next words. "You do know that my last name is Peterson, right?"

Aidan's eyes widen. "You're a Peterson?"

"Born and raised," I say, lifting my chin and sticking my chest out. But then I push my shoulders forward, pulling my chest back in, because I'm sure I look ridiculous, like my defiant two-year-old nephew, Jonathan. "And those 'obnoxious' women that run the place" — I know I'll be embarrassed later when I remember that I used a super whiny voice and air quotes when I said *obnoxious* — "are my mother and aunt."

"Oh," is all he says, his face dropping slightly.

I sit there, looking at him, doing that eyebrow raise as if to say, *And? Don't you have something else to say?*

A normal person would apologize, right away. They might even do a bit of groveling. I'd definitely do some backtracking if the tables were turned. But not Aidan St. Claire. He's got a scowl on his face that suggests he doesn't regret the fact that I'm a Peterson and he's just insulted my family farm to my face.

"You're not going to apologize?"

"Well, I . . ."

I hold out a hand to stop him. I can't believe the nerve of this guy. And to think, I found him attractive. I was wrong about him. He's not just emotionally unavailable. Aidan St. Claire is a jackass.

"Never mind," I say as I stand up from my chair. "I'm leaving now."

Crap. I wish I would have just left instead of announcing it. I'm not going to allow myself to worry about that, because this will be the last time I ever see him.

Thank goodness.

Chapter Seven

Jenna Peterson's Guide to Dating Emotionally Unavailable Men:

You'll replay a lot of conversations in your mind and dwell on lots of things you wish you would have or could have said. Try not to waste your brainpower on it.

My encounter with Aidan is still playing in my mind as I work at the farm the next day. I have so many things I wanted to say or wish I had said. So many fantastic verbal punches. Some of them were below the belt, and even in my imagination I felt bad about those. It doesn't matter, because it's too late now. Unless I want to call him up to call him out—which, believe me, I've thought about.

I'm so agitated that when Josie asked me about it, I blew her off. She gave me her teacher face of concern, but I didn't want to talk to her about it, and I usually want to tell Josie everything.

The problem is, now his words taunt me. Every time I've heard someone say *pumpkiny* today, I've flinched. I haven't joined in when everyone yells *pumpkin* at the top of each hour. The sisters even seem extra over-the-top today. Like more than they usually are. I even hate my hat more, which I didn't think was possible. I'm annoyed by this. It's as if Aidan St. Claire has tainted my family farm. I don't want his words to do that for Josie, too. So I couldn't tell her.

This is the first time I've heard negativity about the farm from an outsider. I'm sure there are other people out there, other customers that agree with him, but I've never met any of them. We've never even gotten a negative Google review — something my dad and uncle pride themselves on. That's why I think it's thrown me for a loop.

"Aren't you supposed to be at the ticketing office?" my sister, Olivia, asks when she finds me at the cider stand. I was hiding, actually. Sitting in that office all day can be boring at times. And I was feeling antsy. Plus, we're nearing the end of the day and entrance tickets are rarely sold at this point.

I love this little cider stand. My dad and uncle built it a couple of years back when the other one was deemed unusable by the sisters. It's a simple wooden structure but looks like a tiny house from the front. It's painted white, with a sign that says *Hot Cider* hanging just above the window where we pass out warm drinks to customers. It smells like a little bit of heaven with that lovely scent of cinnamon filling the space and the surrounding area.

I should remind Aidan St. Claire of the cider. He couldn't have a bad thing to say about that. Or perhaps he could. Gah. He's so annoying.

"I put Brayden on it," I say. He's one of the teenagers we hire to work during the busy season. There are a lot of them around here — so many that I don't know all their names.

I look at my sister, holding hands with her two-year-old son, Jonathan, looking like she hasn't helped out at all today judging by her hair, makeup, and clothes. Even her orange beret looks classier than mine. And it's the same freaking beret. I'm not sure how she does it—keeping up appearances like she and her family do. Do they bring a change of clothing with them? Are they just so uptight that not even dirt wants to be near them?

She and I are so different; she's like my mom, but on steroids, and I'm more like my dad. Inquisitive and a little disorganized.

I come out from the booth and squat down on my heels so I'm eye level with Jonathan.

"Hey there, buddy," I say, giving him a bright smile. I hold up a fist for him to bump, which he ignores.

"Girls have vaginas," he says in reply.

My smile falls. "That's . . . right," I say, giving my sister a *what-the-hell* look, the corner of my lip curling upward as my brows pull down. She answers with a quick shrug.

The kid has an impressive vocabulary for being nearly two and a half—I'll give him that. I'm not sure why he needs to learn about anatomy at this age but leave it to my sister to make sure he's properly educated and using the right wordage. No "hoo-has" or "ding-a-lings" or "private parts" for her. I shouldn't be surprised. Her oldest son, my nephew Lucas, is six, and her middle daughter, my niece Genevieve, is four. This proper education thing has been going on for some time.

Just like the professional organizing business she runs, she's also got her life arranged just how she wants it. All three of Olivia's kids are almost exactly two years apart, all born in the first part of April, all potty trained by eighteen months, and all show signs of being future candidates for Mensa. They all find my humor juvenile, no matter how many pig noses and fart jokes I've thrown their way. The fart jokes are mostly to annoy my sister, who apparently has no gastrointestinal tract, since she's never let one rip in her entire life, or so she would have us think. It's hard to believe she was raised on a farm.

"Where's Regi?" I ask as I stand up after giving Jonathan my best pig nose and a few oinks, which doesn't even elicit a smile from him. I always call Reginald Kingsley Gilbert III (his actual name) Regi, knowing full well that my sister will either call me out or give me a dirty look for not using her husband's full first name. I aim to annoy, like a little sister should.

Ooooh, she's scrunching her nose and deepening the spot between her brows, which is starting to leave a permanent mark. I've warned her all her scowling will only make her look older faster, but she usually quips back with another scowl and a comment about how there's always Botox. Time for her to start exploring that avenue. Should I tell her? Nah. I don't really feel up to it right now.

"Reginald," she overpronounces his name, "is with Lucas and Genevieve, helping out at the maze," she says.

Does she know that nicknames are all the rage right now? Why not Luke, or Eve, or—heaven forbid—Jon? Even Jonny would do. But we must use their full names at all times. Reginald, Olivia, Lucas, Genevieve, and Jonathan. I wonder, if I counted up all the milliseconds it takes to say everyone's full names, if, in a lifetime, an entire day is wasted. Life is too short for long names. My kids, if I ever have any, will have fun and easy names. Like Kate. I've always liked that name. And if they get my genes, they won't be anywhere close to Mensa, and I will love them just the same.

"Anyway, Mom's looking for you," she says.

"Great," I say sarcastically and mostly under my breath.

"There you are." My mom walks toward us, as if our speaking about her has summoned her out of thin air. This has happened more than once, and I'm beginning to be a little suspicious. My mother could, in fact, be a witch.

"Hey, Mom," I say, acknowledging the tiny woman. Jonathan, who couldn't show me an ounce of happiness, gives my mom a big smile and wraps his little arms around her leg when she stops in front of us. She reaches down and tousles his hair, which Olivia is quick to put right.

Dana Peterson has on her orange Peterson's Pumpkin Patch T-shirt and her beret just like the rest of us. Only Olivia has paired hers with a tailored pencil skirt, which looks ridiculous.

Usually my mom and my aunt Lottie are joined at the hip around the farm during the season. But since Lottie is having an existential crisis over Josie and her pirate, she's been hiding behind the scenes more.

"I'm glad I found you. I need you to think of something to help raise money for the barn," my mom says to me. She and my aunt have been really pushing the donation thing because neither my dad nor Uncle Charles would do it. Neither of them is good at asking for help.

"Me?" I point to myself.

"Yes," she says. "I don't know if we'll make it with the donations. I thought so at first, but this past week they've slowed down significantly. Can you think of some ideas?"

I'm kind of taken aback by this. My mom always turns to Olivia for this kind of stuff, never me. I feel bad now that I thought she was a witch.

"Sure," I say, feeling a little pang of love in my heart for her right now. And also a bit smug toward Olivia. Look who's asking me for help and not you.

"I've got some working ideas," says Olivia.

"Thank you, Sweet," she says. "I knew you'd be up for the task."

My smugness dies as my pang of love falls to my feet. I'm just another person on that witch Dana Peterson's list. Makes sense.

"Okay, I'm off to check on the bunnies," she says, prying little Jonathan's arms off her legs, and with a little wave she's off.

Olivia gives me a curt nod, as sisters do. I actually don't know what normal sisters do. But that's Olivia's and my relationship right there in a nutshell: one curt nod. She then grabs Jonathan by the hand, and without a word, they walk away.

"Bye, lady with a vagina," Jonathan yells at me as they go, my sister giving him a stern look, which only serves to scare the poor kid. How dare he embarrass her in public like that. Serves her right for birthing supergeniuses.

"Hey, that's aunt with a vagina to you, mister," I yell back. It stops a few people in their tracks. I feel a pang at justifying Aidan St. Claire's assessment of the farm in that moment.

Chapter Eight

Jenna Peterson's Guide to Dating Emotionally Unavailable Men:

Don't expect apologies. They are about as frequent as actual sightings of bigfoot.

I turn and walk back toward the ticketing office. My mind on the barn and ways we can get the money we need for it. I may not have been top of my mom's list for help, but she did ask me. And I do want to help our family. I'd put more of my own money in, if I could. But I live paycheck to paycheck at this point, with very little extra to spend. I may work at an expensive spa in a ritzy area, but that doesn't always translate to a lot of money. Especially since fall isn't our busy season in Aspen Lake. We're mainly a summer and winter kind of town. And I don't get paid to work on the farm. That is a family obligation. I'm still paying off my debt to my mother for having to birth and raise me. A fact she brings up often.

Since it's practically closing time, I should probably get started on my duties, which include tallying all the day's sales up so I can report them to my family. I do this on the weekends while my dad does it the rest of the week. Luckily, we do everything by computer, so it doesn't take much time, but the donation jar has added some extra work. I don't mind, though. I'm grateful for everyone who's helped out with rebuilding the barn. I just wish I could think of something else I could do.

What a scary day that was, when the barn housing all the corncribs burned down. We still don't know how it started. At least there were no casualties. No one was severely hurt, save my uncle Charles, who broke his leg trying to help put the fire out. He's still sporting a limp to prove it.

I enter the small orange building that's like my home on the weekend; the smell of old wood and paper welcome me as I plop down in the chair at the front desk and swivel around to the small space heater and flick it on. The evenings are starting to cool off quickly as we get closer to October, and the chill is seeping into this room. Only five more weekends before Halloween, when we officially close and I can go back to having my time to myself to . . . well, hang out by myself, I guess. Now that Josie's locking lips with Reece and I've given up on men, I'll have a lot of time on my hands.

At least I'll get to spend more time at home, in the little condo I rent in Aspen Lake. I lucked out and was able to rent a place from a friend, and she's giving me a killer deal on it. She just wanted someone to take care of it for her, someone who wouldn't trash it. The kitchen had just been renovated before she rented it to me. It's in a great location, near the ski slopes, and the best part is, it was left mostly furnished. My favorite piece is the pink velvet couch in the living room. It's the most perfect place to curl up. Not that I've done much of that since moving in.

I take off my beret and get down to business, spending the next half hour adding up the sales and shooting off an email with today's total to my dad. Then, blowing air out my cheeks,

I slide the donation jar over so it's right in front of me. It's only half-full today, which makes my stomach do a little sinking thing. It feels like a far-off dream that we'll get the barn rebuilt, and a lot of our income normally comes from that barn.

I start pulling bills out and putting them in piles. As soon as I'm getting into my groove, there's a soft knock on the guest window, which I closed to keep the cold air out. I'm not sure who it is, but anyone in my family wouldn't knock like that. They wouldn't knock at all, actually. They'd just yell through the glass. I lean closer to the window and am taken aback when I recognize the face of Aidan St. Claire.

What's he doing here? I was never supposed to see him again. And now he's here on my *obnoxious* farm? I scowl at the window, giving him my best Olivia Peterson Gilbert mean face. She's perfected the craft—many a person has been frightened by her glare. I'm still an apprentice, apparently, because Aidan doesn't seem affected in the slightest. I stand up from my chair and slide the window open.

"Come here to sling more insults at my family farm?"

He shakes his head. "No."

"Then what are you doing here? Did you come here to buy a pumpkin? Try to find some fall spirit?" I'm so confused right now.

He lets out a breath. "I came to apologize." His voice is gruff, but there's another tone to it this time. Sincerity.

He's come all this way to apologize? I pull my head back in disbelief. It was a rare occasion when any of the last four men I dated could say they were sorry. Not until they'd opened up. At least they were all fully capable of apologizing when they broke up with me. *I'm sorry, Jenna, but . . .*

"Okay, then say it."

He scrunches his nose. "I thought I just did."

"You said you came to apologize, but you didn't actually say the words *I'm sorry*."

I'm being petty here, I realize. It feels a lot like stooping to his level, and I'm kind of relishing in it.

"Okay, I'm sorry."

"For what?"

He lets out a frustrated breath. "For offending your family's farm."

"But are you sorry for what you said?"

He rolls his lips inward, his shoulders falling a bit. He doesn't have to say it; I can tell by his look. He stands by what he said, but he's sorry it hurt me.

"See you later, Aidan," I say, reaching up to shut the window.

"Wait," he says. "I . . . wanted to talk to you about something."

"I'm sorry, I've got too many pumpkiny things to do right now." I gesture at the money lain out in front of me, overemphasizing the word *pumpkiny* and feeling a pang of annoyance that it still gives me an icky feeling when I say it. This makes me even more irritated at the man standing outside the guest entrance window. It's *his* fault I feel that way.

"Please?" he asks, his tone pleading.

I blow air out my nose. "Okay, but you have to come inside." I point to the door that's on the side of the building. "This place cools off fast with this window open."

He nods and then turns and walks toward the door. I open it after letting him stand there for a bit—still rolling with my petty theme—and feel the cold air rush in as he steps inside. He's wearing dark jeans, and his hands are tucked into a black

North Face jacket. His dark hair is combed back, like he just did it, and the red of his cheeks from the cold makes his crystal-blue eyes pop even more. I really hate that he's pretty. The only good to come from last night is that even though I can acknowledge he's attractive, I can honestly say I don't feel anything for him. Not a smidgen of warmth. I don't even think his forearms would do anything for me. I'm not ready to test that theory, though, so I hope he keeps his jacket on.

Without saying anything to him, I move to the counter and get back to my money organizing, continuing to straighten out the wadded-up bills and separating them into piles. There are way more one-dollar bills than anything else. I'm grateful for it. Every little bit helps.

"Going through the donation jar?" Aidan asks, by way of conversation, after standing there and staring for a bit. I wasn't about to start the conversation off like I normally would, even if it feels uncomfortable. I kind of hope he'll just give up and walk away. Although, I am slightly curious about what he wants to talk to me about.

"Yep," I say, putting the dollar bills into piles of ten. "Look how many people appreciate my family farm." I gesture with my hand at all the money in front of me.

He sighs. "I'm sure they do. Will you meet your goal?"

"I don't know," I say, my tone curt. "It will probably take a miracle."

If only I could figure out a way to earn the money we need so that I can throw it into Olivia's face and give my mom something to be proud of. It would be such a win-win.

"Okay, so what do you need to talk to me about?" I ask.

"Right," he says. I glance over at him and catch him licking his lips in a sort of nervous way. "I . . . I was wondering if you could help me."

This makes me stop what I'm doing and turn toward him fully. "Help you," I repeat. What on earth would Aidan St. Claire need my help with? He's got a lot of nerve, this guy.

"Yeah," he says and then clears his throat.

"Okay, I'll bite," I say. "What do you need help with?"

He looks over to the side, clearing his throat again. It's clear that he doesn't know how to say what he wants to say. Unfortunately for him, I ran out of all the craps I can give today, so I'm not going to help him.

I'm just about to go back to counting, since the silence is making me feel twitchy, and then he opens his mouth. "The woman I brought here," he says. "The one that put the money in the jar."

"Yeah?"

"She broke up with me that night, after our visit to the farm."

"Oh, is it because you weren't being pumpkiny enough for her?" I tilt my head to the side, giving him my best smirk. I don't know how his girlfriend breaking up with him has anything to do with me, but I couldn't help the dig.

"Something like that," he says.

"What do you mean?"

He clears his throat. "She said I'm like talking to a brick wall."

This makes me snort out a laugh. That's a great way to describe Aidan. "Sorry," I say when I see that it's not so funny to him. "Let me guess, you weren't open enough for her?"

He doesn't say anything—he just nods.

"Shocking," I say sarcastically.

"I've . . . uh, gotten this a lot. The brick wall thing. Not exactly in those same words, though."

I just nod my head, so many snide remarks sitting on the edge of my tongue, but I hold them in. I can imagine that's a common theme in his life—people telling him he's hard to talk to. Because he is.

"So, what does this have to do with me?"

"Before I insulted your family farm"—his face contorts a bit when he says this, sort of like a tiny cringe—"we seemed to be having a pretty good conversation."

"Yeah," I say, recalling the feeling I had—the one where I was quite proud of myself for getting him to talk. It felt like a reward of sorts. That was until he screwed it all up.

"You said it's your thing, getting people to open up."

I lift my shoulders and let them drop. "So?"

"You said if I needed help, you could do it."

I chortle. "Aidan, I told you I was kidding." Why did I even say that? *I'm your gal.* Just thinking those words sends an uncomfortable tingle down my spine. Someone needs to invent that back arrow button for me, stat. I could rewind all the way back to the invitation to the bar and change my reply to *No freaking way.*

He licks his lips. "I know you said you were kidding. But—" he cuts off, letting out a heavy sigh. His eyes move toward the ceiling. It's the kind of eye roll you do when you feel frustrated or maybe stupid, a quick one with a little head shake added for emphasis.

He squares his shoulders after that, takes a breath, and moves his line of sight back to me. "I have to be at this big boat expo thing the second week of November in Vegas. It only happens every four years, and my company is a big sponsor—we have been for decades. My grandpa was always the one to do it, even after he was basically retired . . . and he was good at it. And now I have to go. I'll need to talk to people. A lot." He tucks a hand into the pocket of his coat. "And, I need help."

"Help . . . talking?"

"Yes. I have to speak to people at the booth we have in the showroom, and there will be dinners with clients and manufacturers, and a big charity gala at the end. And possibly some golfing." He reaches up and rubs his forehead, like just thinking about this is overwhelming to him.

I stare at him for a few beats, the sound of the space heater filling the room. "Couldn't you send someone else? To the boat show thing?" I ask.

He shakes his head. "It has to be me. We have a reputation in the industry I need to uphold. I don't want to mess it up. I *can't* mess it up."

"And you think I can help?" I'm definitely digging those lines between my brows super deep right now with all the confused looks I'm giving him. Botox is in my future. I can't help myself—even if the aesthetician in me is cringing right now. This entire conversation is so . . . *weird.*

He shrugs. "I'm hoping."

I huff out a breath. "Wouldn't a therapist be better at helping you with this?"

"I've tried that."

"A life coach?"

"I've never worked with one."

"Why me?" I ask out of curiosity. "It's not like we had some crazy deep discussion yesterday."

"I felt comfortable with you. I told you things I've never told anyone else. Like the lucky charm thing. I . . . I wanted to tell you more about myself. That's"—he stops to swallow— "not the norm for me."

And the toxic trait strikes again.

I twist my lips to the side as many thoughts go through my mind. Mainly how weird this is, him asking me for help. I'll give him this: he's got a lot of gumption after our conversation yesterday.

"So, let me get this straight," I finally say. "You insult my family farm, and now you want my help?" I feel a little Godfather-ish with that last line. *You insult my family . . .*

"I . . ." His shoulders drop. "I really am sorry about that."

To his credit, he does seem sincere. But is he only being sincere because he wants my help? Gah. This man is so frustrating.

"This is all super strange, Aidan," I say.

"I know."

"I wouldn't even know where to begin. This isn't like a job I do or something."

He looks down at the ground, his hand still in his coat pocket. "I'm only asking you to try."

He's only asking me to try. Why would I even want to?

"What's in it for me?" I fold my arms, stepping one foot forward and leaning on my back leg. There's a 99.9 percent chance I'm going to say no to this ridiculousness, but I ask this out of curiosity.

Aidan's eyes dart around the room. I'm assuming he didn't think we'd get to this part, or that I'd even want something in return. Typical man.

His eyes land on the donation jar sitting on the counter. Then they quickly move to me. "I'll give you money for the barn," he says. "Five grand."

"Five thousand dollars?" I eke out as my mouth literally falls open. If I were a cartoon, my jaw would have hit the floor. *What?* "That . . . that's a lot of money."

"I'm good for it," he says.

I'm totally taken aback by this. I keep opening my mouth, trying to form a sentence, but am only able to sputter out half words. "Bu . . . ho . . . wha . . .?" However, three fully formed and distinct words keep running through my brain: *five thousand dollars.*

That money could be huge for the barn. I could contribute in a big way. My mom would be so impressed. I might even move from being the black sheep of the family to a more dark-gray color.

"What if it doesn't work?" I say, finally able to use real words. *Good job, Jenna.*

Aidan gives me big eyes, like this was a confirmation from me. It wasn't exactly. But I've gone from a 99.9 percent chance of saying no to 25 percent. For five thousand reasons.

"You'll do it?"

"I don't know," I say, and his face falls a little. "There's not that much time until November. And what if it's more than just opening up and talking? What if it's like a social phobia or something?"

He shakes his head. "I don't have a problem being around people. I just don't always know how to talk to them. I know it's a long shot," he says. His hands are out of his pockets and are now both pointed toward me, palms up. "I'll still pay, even if it doesn't help me. But . . . I need to try something."

The room is silent again as we stare at each other. This is starting to sound like an offer I can't refuse. Even if the man standing before me insulted my family farm, and even if I have no idea what I'll actually do to help him. But I have to try, right?

Chapter Nine

Jenna Peterson's Guide to Dating Emotionally Unavailable Men:

The key to getting someone to open up is to meet them on their level. Find out their interests and know that you will likely find them boring.

I said yes.

How could I not? This will be huge for my family. It's like the universe is finally giving me a win for once.

I realized an added bonus, as I was falling asleep last night, that this will be a great distraction for me. True, it's in the same vein as what I was trying to avoid in the first place, but this time I'm helping out an emotionally unavailable man who I have *zero* feelings for.

I've finally recognized my Achilles' heel with men: if they insult my family, it zaps any and all feelings for them. It's been so long since this has happened, I'd completely forgotten. But last night I remembered that back in high school when my big crush—Tripp Collins, the quarterback for the football team—teased Josie about being the *pirate girl*, he was immediately dead to me. All feelings for him were gone. Poof. Just like that. In fact, any boy that called her that—which was most boys, because high school is rough—were on the *Jenna No List*. It left me a very small dating pool. Which could be how my career in serial dating emotionally challenged men started. That's a lot to think about. Maybe I won't unpack all that right now.

I did feel the need to warn Aidan about my nonfeelings last night. Which proved to be a little awkward.

"Okay, I'll help you," I'd said, after making him squirm a little while I mulled over my options. Really, once the $5,000 was on the table, it was a no-brainer.

He'd let out a big breath before saying, "Okay, great," with about as much gusto as someone finding out they have a bunion. Was it wrong to expect even just a tiny bit of enthusiasm?

I decided I don't need him to be a cheerleader. I've got $5,000 doing that for me. *Gooooo, Jenna!*

We spent some time trying to figure out how this was all going to happen since we're up against a deadline, and as I had previously stated, this is not something I've got a manual for.

"There's just one caveat," I'd said after we'd discussed what our first plan of action would be, which was dinner the next night. "This whole thing isn't going to be like dating." I pointed a finger at myself and then at Aidan. "And I will absolutely not fall for you."

"Okay," he'd said, his brows pulling downward.

"I just needed you to know that, in case you . . . wondered."

"I didn't expect . . . that's . . . sure, okay," he'd fumbled over his words.

In hindsight, I could have left that whole part out and just kept it to myself—the not falling for him thing. But I'd said it, it was embarrassing, and now I'm going to have to suffer through replaying it in my head for the rest of my life because that's just how these kinds of things go for me.

Once, at the previous spa I worked at before moving to Aspen Lake, I asked the owner of the place—a very stoic and quiet man—if he was having a good morning, but instead of *morning*, I said *horny*. As in: *Are you having a good horny?* There's not been a day that goes by that I don't think about that.

Currently I find myself in my cute condo, getting ready for the dinner we planned, having all sorts of thoughts run through my brain. Most of them are in the doubtful category. Like, *How am I going to do this?* Or, *Am I* really *going to do this?*

I had a lot of time to think about it today, since it was slower than usual for a Sunday at the farm. This isn't so great for our bottom line at Peterson's Pumpkin Patch, but it did give me a chance to work up a plan of sorts for Aidan. I even wrote a list in my phone. It's titled: *How to Help Aidan St. Claire Not Be a Jackass.*

I started my research by doing what pretty much anyone does in this day and age: I googled.

Each of my searches produced a slew of articles. I started with "How to get someone to open up." This was fascinating because nothing from those articles was surprising. They were all things I've unintentionally done in the past. It's all about getting the person to feel safe, to know they are with someone who's trustworthy. Then asking questions and offering sympathy and understanding. It's Good Listening 101, essentially. Give people the right opportunities to open up, and they will.

The best way to do this I've found—and confirmed by Google—is to discover their interests and do them together.

And then ply them with questions the whole time. I'm a pro at this.

For example, Matthew was into cars, so for him, long drives were a great way to chat. For Garrett, it was poetry slams. After one of those, he'd be so hopped up on adrenaline, he'd open right up.

For Cam it was doing something adventurous. Like rock climbing. He'd be an open book once we got to the top. As for Brian, he liked to go fishing. So that's what we did. I learned a lot about him as we sat in the two-person fishing boat on the quiet Aspen Lake. I learned a lot about myself, too, during all this, like the fact that I don't love fishing. Or poetry slams.

The problem with Aidan isn't getting him to open up to me as much as helping him to talk to strangers. To be normal in a people-y setting. Google was not so helpful with this one. What came up in a search was mostly articles about how you can't force someone to talk if they don't want to, and how you shouldn't pressure them into doing it if it's not their thing. I felt a little chastised by the internet. But it's not like I'm forcing him to do this; he asked me.

So my plan tonight is to have dinner with Aidan and get to know him better. Then set up some things we can do, based on possible interests he has that will help him feel comfortable, and then we'll practice ways to talk to people. I have no idea if this will work, but it's all I've got. Then beyond that, I have an idea that I hope he'll agree to. I won't be telling him what it is tonight, though. I don't want to scare the poor guy.

The best part about this whole thing is: Aidan and I aren't dating. As I so eloquently pointed out last night. There will be no physical anything. I won't have to carefully pull back layers like I have in the past. We can jump right in.

All day at the farm, I kept wanting to tell my family about the money Aidan is going to give me, but I never could. Even with Josie. Luckily for me, her head is up in the clouds with Reece the Pirate right now, and so we mostly talked about her.

The truth is, I don't want to get anyone's hopes up and have it fail. I know he said he'd pay me either way, but it feels like it's too good to be true. And my dad always said that if it seems too good to be true, it probably is. But I have to take the chance, right? And Aidan, for all that I know of him, doesn't seem like the kind of man that would go back on his word. He doesn't say things out the side of his mouth. He can barely say things out the front of it.

My other reason for not telling anyone is because I couldn't think of a way to explain myself without sounding like a crazy person. *I'm going to help a man try to be more open, and he's going to pay me to do it.* The sisters would most likely interpret that to mean that I've become a sex worker, and no matter how hard I'd try to talk them down, they wouldn't be deterred. Once they set their mind to something, it's hard to bring them back. Josie knows this all too well. That pirate story was never going to die, and now that she's dating the inspiration for it, our moms will probably be talking about it even from their graves.

So when my mom checked in today to see if I'd come up with any ideas, I'd said, "Yes, I think I have."

"Wonderful. What ideas?" she'd asked.

"I have one that I think will work. I just need to figure out some of the details." I surprised myself with my off-the-cuff answer.

"Okay," she'd said and then gave me her closed-mouth smile of disappointment. I've gotten that look quite a few times in my life.

She won't be disappointed when I present her with the money from Aidan. But first, I need to actually get myself ready to go to this dinner. After showering and finding my favorite pair of jeans, which were on the floor under a pile of clothes I've been meaning to fold, I throw on a cable-knit ivory sweater and put on a bit of makeup. I'm going for a not-trying-too-hard look, but still nice enough since Aidan has so far only seen me in my orange Peterson's Pumpkin Patch T-shirt or scrubs. Not that I want him to see me in other clothes—it will just be nice to not look like I'm at work.

I take a look in the mirror hanging over the small table near the front door of my place, fluff my dark-blond hair up, clean up a little eyeliner smudge under my eye, and then give myself a quick pep talk. I take a deep breath and then head to my car, wishing I'd brought a jacket, but not enough to go back, as I walk in the cold night air to my dark-blue sedan.

On the drive over, despite my pep talk, I can't help the nervousness that settles over me. And the worry that I won't be able to do this. I mean, I probably won't be able to. And I know myself: I won't take the money if I fail. It will feel like cheating. Then this will all be a waste of my time. I'm pretty much questioning everything. I think the thought of $5,000 and what it could do for my family may have jumbled my brain.

I'm so worked up by the time I arrive at the restaurant, I've come up with a completely different plan. And that is to tell Aidan I've changed my mind.

But after valeting the car and following the host to a table that's in the far back corner of the restaurant, I sit across from Aidan, with his back ramrod straight, his quick and curt thank-you to the host after clearing his throat multiple times, his inability to say hello to me—possibly from his own nervousness— I change my mind back. This guy needs me. Also, I'm feeling ravenous and it smells amazing in here, like garlic and butter. That also might have played into my decision.

"So," I say by way of greeting. Aidan's nervousness has me feeling my own less, so I sit back in my chair and take the perfectly folded white linen napkin off the plate in front of me and place it in my lap.

"Thank you for coming," Aidan says.

I just give him a nod, because what else can I say? *Thank you for $5,000.* That would make him think I'm only doing this for the money. Which I am. And he probably knows that.

He clears his throat, and I sniffle for no reason. We are off to a stellar start. Also, I'm doing that cold-sweating thing. So maybe I'm still a little nervous.

I take in a breath, steadying myself, and look around me. We're at a restaurant called The Lake, which is a steak house that sits on a cliff above the glorious crystal-blue water this town is known for. We're sitting on the east side, which is an entire wall of windows. The rest of the walls are covered in dark wood paneling, the overhead lighting dim. Round tables with stark-white tablecloths are dotted throughout the large dining room, each with a lighted votive candle in a speckled gold glass holder sitting in the center.

Not every table is full, but there are plenty of patrons in the upscale establishment. The low murmur of people talking and cutlery on plates can be heard, as well as soft classical music in the background.

"Nice table," I say. I look out the window, the moon hanging low, just peeking above the trees of the mountains surrounding the lake, its light shining a pathway on the still water.

"It's my regular one," he says in that gruff tone of his. It's growing on me. It's sort of Vin Diesel meets Oscar the Grouch.

"Right," I say. I should have realized, when he so easily offered me five grand to help him, that Aidan probably comes from a long line of money. That happens when your family's company sells boats. When Josie's and my parents die, they will leave us . . . a farm. Not a super lucrative one either. And they will expect us to run it, or at least one of the four Peterson offspring. I'm pretty sure the sisters will haunt us if we don't.

It hasn't been said or put in writing, but the farm will probably become Oliver's responsibility at some point. Not that the farm has to go to the firstborn son or anything, but because he's the one who's shown the most interest. He's practically been campaigning for the job. I don't think he'll get much pushback from the rest of us on that one either.

"What's good here?" I ask Aidan, while perusing the menu and wondering what chiffonade is. I don't want to ask and sound like an idiot. So I'll just hope it's nothing scary.

Aidan clears his throat a couple of times before saying, "The filet is excellent."

"I'll have that, then," I say as I place my menu on the table.

This must be a cue for the server because she appears just seconds after, bringing with her a bottle of wine Aidan apparently picked out before I arrived. She shows it to us, opens it, pours a small bit for Aidan, who takes a drink and contemplates it before nodding, and then pours us each a glass.

"I hope the wine is okay," he says, gesturing to me with his hand, once the server has taken our orders and leaves us to ourselves. "You could order a Coke."

"This is fine," I say, giving him a quick nod. I take a sip, and it tastes expensive. And also, not terrible.

It's silent again, save for the quiet rumble from the other people in the room. I suppose it's my job to get things started, since Aidan has already declared — and made pretty obvious — that he's not so good at this.

"How was your day?" I ask him.

"Good," he says, giving me his normal quick and short answer.

"Did you do anything?"

"Caught up on some work."

"And what was that?"

"Just work."

I purse my lips. "You're going to need to give me more than that."

He reaches up and rubs his temples. "I'm not good at small talk."

"I know," I say, giving him a closed-mouth smile. "How about you try relaxing a bit. You look like you're sitting in a classroom rather than a five-star restaurant." I gesture around the main dining room with my hand.

He lets out a slow breath. "I'm nervous," he says.

"Me too," I say, and his eyes meet mine. They are pretty under the dim lighting, with those thick black eyelashes.

"You don't look like you are," he says.

I lift my shoulders briefly. "I'm good at hiding it."

"So how is this all going to work? You helping me."

"Look at you. You said more than six words in one sentence," I say, giving him my best wry smile.

He does that thing, where the corners of his mouth move up his face, ever so slightly. It's . . . not ugly. "I'm trying," he says.

I place my forearms on the edge of the table and weave my hands together. "Since I've never done this kind of thing, I looked up some ideas, and I made a list of sorts," I tell him.

"A list?"

"Yes," I say. "I thought we could start by finding out what you like to do."

His brows pull downward. "Why do you need to know that?"

"Because," I say. "I've found that it's sometimes easier to talk when you're doing something you enjoy. Like a hobby or something."

He gives me a curious stare. Oh gosh, what if there is nothing Aidan St. Claire likes to do? What if he's one of those work types that has nothing extracurricular. Then what will I do? My whole plan starts with this.

"Uh . . . golf," he says.

Excellent. He's not one of those types. I can work with this.

"That's perfect, since you might have to do that at the conference, right?"

"I was planning on getting out of that one."

"Why?"

"I don't like to talk a lot when I golf."

"How do you know you don't like to talk?"

"I've gone with other people before and there wasn't much talking."

"From everyone? Or just you?"

"Just me."

"Okay," I say. "What else do you like to do?"

"I like to go hiking sometimes when the weather is nice," he says.

"That's a good one," I say.

"I also go sailing sometimes," he says.

"Owner of a boating company, that makes sense," I say with a nod. "I've never been, actually."

"It's a good way to get my mind off things," he says, looking down at the candlelight flickering between us.

"That's perfect. And have you hiked before with anyone else? Or sailed?"

Aidan reaches up and rubs his jaw with his thumb and pointer finger. "I take my mom sailing with me sometimes," he says.

"What about any colleagues?"

"Not really."

"Your brother?"

His eyes dart to mine, and there's something behind them this time. Something a little jarring. The way he blinks, almost purposefully, like he's reminding himself to do it, and the way his jaw twitches on the left side. "Never," he says.

Right. Got it. I can read the body language loud and clear. Someone standing on the moon could probably read it. Note to self: don't bring up the brother. Not yet, at least, because of course I'm now quite curious.

I think about it for a second. This is going to be harder than I thought. "I think we should try golfing."

His brows pull downward again. "I already told you, I'm going to get out of that," he says.

"But what if you can't?"

He looks out the window, staring at the lake below. "I don't know."

"Shouldn't we try?"

He swallows, giving me a look like I have two heads. "Are you sure this is the best way? To . . . to help me?"

"Do you have a better plan in mind?" I ask, feeling sort of defensive. I don't know if this is the best way, because I've never done this before. I've never mindfully tried to help someone be more open—it's just something I can usually do. And I for sure have never worked with someone to help them talk to other people. We are the blind leading the blind here.

He shakes his head. "No, I don't."

"Then let's try this and see what happens," I say. "If it doesn't work, then we'll try another way."

He lets out a breath. "Okay."

"Okay," I say. I reach up and rub the side of my head, feeling an ache settling there. Probably because I'm unconsciously gritting my teeth right now.

I've certainly got my work cut out for me.

Chapter Ten

Jenna Peterson's Guide to Dating Emotionally Unavailable Men:

Hone those conversational skills, and be prepared for one-word answers like, yeah, uh-huh, and okay.

Heaven help me, golf is so boring. I might be adding this to my list of activities I don't like, just under fishing and above slam poetry. The jury is still out, though. I've done this a few times before and don't remember it being so boring. It could be that I've forgotten, or it's also possible that golfing with Aidan St. Claire is what's boring. He said he didn't like to talk when he golfed, and he wasn't kidding. He will definitely *not* be able to do this at the conference.

It's Tuesday and we both got out of work early. Me, because I had a clear schedule for the afternoon, no facials to do. And Aidan, because he's the boss. So we met up at the Blue Lake Golf Course, which I've never been to.

What a waste of an afternoon. I didn't bother bringing my dad's clubs because I wasn't planning on golfing. I was just going to walk with Aidan while he did. I figured we'd have time to chat while walking to the next shot. We decided not to rent a cart because we're playing a smaller course and Aidan prefers to walk. I could use the exercise myself, since I've missed my last couple of workouts.

But because it's a smaller course, it doesn't take quite as long to walk to the next shot, and so there just isn't that much time. We'll make small talk, and then I'll ask a deeper question, and Aidan will take some time to think about his answer before we arrive at the ball, and then he'll forget about my question because his mind is now on the shot and what club he wants to use. Then after the shot, he'll say, "What were we talking about?" And rinse and repeat.

Since I'm not playing and Aidan's not talking, I've had a lot of time to think about things. Like the fact that I'm an idiot for agreeing to do this and how I've already failed. At one point, when I felt that uncomfortable feeling move through my body for the hundredth time—the one I used to get on the first day of school, or on the first day of a new job—I considered just telling him this wasn't going to work and then leaving. But I haven't built up the gumption quite yet. It's been nearly four hours and we're on the last hole—I've made it this far.

I have gotten him to say a handful of comments like: *yes, no, maybe, probably, I guess, not sure,* and *I doubt it.* And if you put all those words together, you'd almost have a full sentence. He'll for sure win over clients or manufacturers with that. I'm killing it.

It is beautiful out today, so at least I have that, with the smell of freshly cut greens on the course, and the mountains and lake in the backdrop. The rows of pine trees on the hills are dotted with aspens turning yellow and the cottonwoods changing to shades of orange. It's a lovely sixty-five degrees, which was a nice bonus because I hadn't even considered the weather when I proposed this joke of an outing.

Even though I'd told him I wasn't going to golf, I did dress for the part, in dark-gray joggers and a light-blue polo, my hair pulled up into a ponytail that hangs over the back of my sun visor.

Aidan showed up in slim-fit stretchy-looking trousers and a white polo that shows off those toned forearms. The clothes fit him like they were tailor-made. He also had on a matching baseball hat . . . and it was on *backward*. I had to swallow, hard. And then try not to look at him. Because holy crap, I am a sucker for a hat on backward. Why is this a thing? Josie and I have had lengthy discussions about this phenomenon. Luckily, once we got out into the sun, he turned the bill to the front.

I take a breath as we walk to what will hopefully be his last shot—if any of the prayers I've been saying are answered, that is. I reach up and rub the ring on my necklace. *Get me out of this, Grandma P.* We're a bit far away and it will take a miracle for him to get it directly into the hole, but that's what I'm praying for. Then we can be done and I can politely tell him that this is impossible—I'm not going to be able to help him.

I'd thought maybe things would be okay today. That he might be more talkative. Last night after we got over our initial awkwardness, he did start to relax and open up a bit.

When I'd said, "This might be the best steak I've ever had," after having taken several bites of the tender filet. I wasn't kidding. It was some of the best food I'd had in my entire life. It was all making sense now, why people are willing to fork out so much money to go to a place like this.

"One of the best," he'd said. "I'm glad you like it."

I'd pulled the napkin out of my lap and dabbed the corners of my mouth like Dana Peterson had taught me to do. I hated all her etiquette training and proper table rules growing up, because they had never once come in handy. Of course, having some decorum while eating is necessary, but does anyone really keep their elbows off the table at a fast-food restaurant? Not in my experience.

But last night, I'd have to hand it to her. I knew which fork was which and was totally able to hold my own. I'll have to thank her someday. Maybe on her deathbed so she can't gloat about it.

"You said this is your normal table; how often do you come here?" I'd asked.

He'd looked thoughtful for a minute. "It used to be more frequent, but probably a couple of times a month, lately," he'd said.

I'd looked around the opulent dining room and wondered how many of the people currently in here were like Aidan, and how many were like me. From the looks of things, I was most likely the odd man out here.

"When did you first start coming?"

"With my grandparents," he'd said. "Many years ago."

"Is it hard to come here? With the memories?" I'd flinched a little when I'd asked this because it was a deeper question and so far we'd only been staying on the surface.

He'd hesitated but then nodded. "At first it was. The table we used to sit at is over there." He'd pointed to the round five-top table sitting on the other end of the window side of the restaurant. The table was empty, just the single votive candle making shadows on the tablecloth.

"But then?" I'd urged him on.

"Then, it became a place I wanted to be for the memories."

"I get that," I'd said. And then, feeling daring, I'd asked him, "Tell me your favorite memory with your grandparents."

The corner of his mouth lifted up just slightly as his eyes looked around the room. "I think one of my favorites was when my grandpa took me sailing for the first time. When I was twelve. It was a fall day on the lake, the wind was perfect, the trees were changing colors."

"Fall is my favorite time of year," I'd interjected. "And not because my family owns a pumpkin farm."

He'd nodded. "I've never thought about it, but it's probably mine too. It was just one of those memories, you know? A good day."

The corners of his lips had turned up higher this time, the dimple on his cheek making an appearance.

I'd felt like we were making some headway, talking the way regular people talk. It felt almost comfortable, almost normal. But now golfing today, I feel like he's back to being his old curmudgeon-ish self. I've rolled my eyes so many times behind his back that I'm starting to feel an ache in my sockets.

He putts the ball into the final hole—my prayer did not come to fruition (*Thanks a lot, Grandma P.*) and it took two more strokes to get here—and I let out a big breath. Finally done. This was a very torturous four hours of my life that I can never get back.

Aidan slides the putter into his bag and pulls the scorecard and pencil out of the pocket of his pants. He scribbles some numbers on it, and then his brow lowers as he studies it.

"Something wrong?" I ask him.

"Hmm," he says, pursing his lips as he looks at the card. "I just golfed an eighty-five." He looks up at me, and I give him a little shrug. He might as well have been speaking German. I have no idea about scoring in golf. I'm not sure we even kept track the other times I've gone.

"That any good?" I ask.

He raises his eyebrows. "It's my best score . . . probably ever."

"Well," I say in a goofy singsong voice, "I must be your good luck charm, then."

He clears his throat, then looks at me and then back at the card. Then he taps the card on his hand a couple of times and his eyes meet mine again. "Can I buy you a drink? At the club?" He tilts his head toward the clubhouse, which is only about fifty yards from us.

How do I nicely say this has been the most boring four hours of my life and I don't think I can extend it a minute longer? And also that I am going to quit trying to do . . . whatever we are doing here. It's not going to work. He's going to have to find another way to communicate at the conference, and I'll just have to do something else to get money for the barn. Perhaps sex working is in my future after all. Or maybe not. I'm not ready for my mom to keel over from disappointment quite yet.

"Yeah, I don't think —"

"Please? I owe you."

Yes, you owe me four hours of my life.

"How do you owe me?" I scrunch my face at him. "We hardly talked. This whole thing" — I gesture toward the green around us — "was pretty much a failure."

His eyes widen, the pupils dilating. "It wasn't a failure for me."

"Aidan, I'm not sure how. You . . . I mean, I should have taken what you said seriously yesterday. You said you didn't talk when you golf. I know you got your best score or whatever, but —"

"That's not what I'm saying."

"Then what are you saying? Because on paper, this wasn't anything like I'd hoped it would be." I wanted to get to know him, to have a dialogue. To understand him better. To, I don't know, maybe then do some role-playing or something. I wasn't able to even get to that part because there was hardly any communication with him.

He breathes out his nose, his mouth closed. He studies my face for a few seconds—long enough that I start to question where my eyes should go. His eyes? His hat? His ear? I settle for staring at his forehead.

"I don't golf with anyone because"—he reaches up and scratches his stubbled jaw—"I feel . . . I don't know . . . anxious, I guess."

"Okay?" I ask him, drawing out the word. What does this have to do with anything?

"I felt that way at first, with you here. But then . . ." He stops talking and looks out at something in the distance and then back at me. "But then, it was good."

It was good? "How?" I ask him.

"How?"

"Yeah, how was it good for me to be trailing you around this entire golf course?"

"It just was. I—" He stops and swallows visibly. "I liked having you here."

"That's not going to help you at the conference," I say.

He reaches up and rubs the back of his neck. "Maybe not for the conference. But it was still helpful to me."

Well, that's something at least.

I look to the sky, exhaling loudly. Then I bring my eyes back to him, shaking my head. This—me coming with him—

was a much bigger deal than I'd thought. I didn't realize that just having another person here was a stretch for him. But I guess it makes sense. Fitting for this guy I'm starting to understand a little better.

"I'm assuming you'll have to get drinks with people at the conference?" I ask.

He blinks a few times while nodding his head. "Of course."

"Fine," I say, begrudgingly. "You can buy me a drink."

"Okay," he says with a quick dip of his chin.

"But none of your one-word answers, okay? You have to try this time."

He swings his clubs onto his shoulder. "I'll do my best," he says.

Chapter Eleven

Jenna Peterson's Guide to Dating Emotionally Unavailable Men:

Emotionally unavailable men are usually quite predictable,
but occasionally, they may surprise you.

We walk over to the clubhouse and I ask Aidan questions
about golf as we do. He's answering them, and not with one-
word sentences, so at least he's trying.

Turns out eighty-five is a really good score for the average
golfer, or at least for someone like Aidan who only plays for
five months of the year—as in, the only months of the year you
can play golf in Aspen Lake. Otherwise, it's too cold or there's
too much snow.

After he drops his bag off with the attendant near the pro
shop, Aidan opens the door for me as we walk inside the main
area of the clubhouse.

I didn't see the building earlier because I just met Aidan by
the tee box of the first hole. So I inhale a little breath when we
walk inside. It's stunning. The large room sports vaulted
ceilings and a mix of light and dark wood paneling all over the
space. There's a large stone fireplace with an older couple
sitting near it, and tables and sitting areas are placed

thoughtfully around the room. The setting sun is shining through the large windows that face the eighteenth hole, where we just were, giving the room a lovely glow with all the natural lighting. There's a square-shaped bar in the south end of the building with high-top chairs tucked in around it.

Aidan follows me inside, and when he puts a hand on the small of my back as we walk to the bar, I take in a quick breath from the shock of it. A tingling sensation crawls up my back. Not in a creepy way, though. I feel like it should be out of character for him to touch me like that, but it almost feels natural. He is a very confusing man. I briefly wonder if I need to give him another awkward talk about how we aren't dating, but then I don't want to jump to conclusions either. It is, after all, just a light touch on my back.

When we get to the counter, he pulls out my chair first and then his own. We're the only people at the bar as we settle in. The bartender, who wasn't there when we first arrived, makes his way to the back side of the bar where there's a little opening, and then he approaches us from the other side of the granite-covered counter. He's a tall man with broad shoulders, dressed in jeans and a white T-shirt with a black unbuttoned vest and a white towel draped over his shoulder.

"What can I get you, Mr. St. Claire?" he asks, giving us both a broad smile.

Aidan looks to me. "I'll have a Coke," I say, taken aback that the bartender clearly knows Aidan.

"I'll have a stout. Thanks, Tom," Aidan tells the bartender. And with a quick nod, Tom goes to the other end of the bar to prepare our drinks.

I cock my head to the side. "Mr. St. Claire?" I ask, using a voice that I had intended to sound extra pompous but really came out as some sort of Regency butler. "You must come here often."

"Not all that often," he says.

"Then how does he know you by name?"

Aidan takes in a breath. "I'm one of the owners."

"Of this golf course?"

He nods just once.

"Can you do that?"

He pulls his chin inward. "What do you mean?"

"Own a golf course."

"Of course. This is a private course, not a municipal one." This makes sense—it's just honestly something I've never thought about.

"So, this clubhouse?" I look around the beautiful room. So perfectly decorated. It's simplistic but still elegant in design.

"Part mine," he says.

"Okay," I say, taken aback and shaking my head as I look around.

"Is that okay?"

My eyes go back to his. "Of course," I say. "Why wouldn't it be?"

"You just seem kind of put off."

"Not at all. I've just never met anyone who owns a golf course."

"Part owner," he clarifies, as Tom the bartender places our drinks in front of us. We thank him before he leaves the bar area.

"Right," I say. "Anything else you mysteriously own?" This feels a little bit like prying, but I can't help myself. I take a sip of my drink, the bubbles tickling my tongue.

"Just some real estate," he says before taking a sip of his beer.

"Is this what you wanted to do? Work for your family and invest and all that?" I bat a hand toward the large dining room behind us.

He glances over his shoulder at the room and then looks back at me. "No," he says. "I wanted to teach high school math and coach football."

I choke on my Coke then. I actually sucked it down the wrong pipe, and I splutter as I try to get myself back in order.

"Are you okay?" he asks, after I've practically heaved up one of my lungs.

"Yes," I say, although my voice is raspy from all the coughing. "You" — I clear my throat — "you just caught me by surprise."

"Why is that so surprising?"

"I don't know, I guess you just don't seem like the type of person who would want to be a teacher."

"Why not? I like kids," he says.

Why do I feel like I want to pat him on the head for that comment? It's kind of adorable. I like kids too. And if it's not in the cards for me to have them, I can be the best aunt ever to my niece and nephews. I'll make them appreciate my fart jokes.

"It's just unexpected, that's all."

"What type do I seem like?"

What job would I picture Aidan having if he hadn't inherited a boating company? Running some massive empire, that's what. He seems like he could command a room with just a look. Not in an alpha-male kind of way but more just because of his quiet, reserved, and . . . well, slightly off-putting nature. He probably scares his employees just by being in their presence. He doesn't even have to say anything. How could someone who mostly gives short and succinct answers teach a high school class? I just can't see it.

Each one of my last four boyfriends had jobs that fit them. By day, Matthew worked in some sort of medical sales, I'm pretty sure. By night, he was an aspiring stand-up comic. I spent many a night in clubs watching open mic competitions. He never won any of them. It's not that he wasn't funny, but it was more of a witty off-the-cuff humor. When he'd planned it out to perform, it became too practiced, too polished sounding. It never seemed to have the effect he was going for.

Brian was the vice president of some big technology company that has an office in Carson City. A big shot kind of job. He definitely fit into that role. I'm sure he was the type of boss that scared people, too. But he wanted to. That's how he ran things. He traveled a lot while we were dating. It was on one of his business trips that he met Gwen, who he's now married to. We were still dating when this happened and I didn't know that detail until after the fact. Supposedly nothing happened until after we were done, but I'm not sure I believe that.

Garrett was a technical writer. He wanted to be a poet, but there isn't a big market out there for that. So he had to make money somehow. On a side note, poetry slams, while not my favorite, are also not all that bad. I thought it'd be weird — like a big cringe fest. And sometimes they were. But it was such a different group of people than what I'm used to. A different breed of human. I don't think I'd choose to go to one on my own, but it was definitely interesting to watch when I went with Garrett. So much drama, so many deep thoughts, so much snapping. You don't clap at a poetry reading. I found this out the hard way. You also don't whistle loudly between your teeth. I'm not upset about it anymore; I'm just saying that information should have been given to me beforehand.

For Cam, well, he was just what you'd imagine someone adventurous would be: a firefighter. Only that kind of job in Carson City isn't exactly fraught with adventure. Most of the calls that came in while he was on duty weren't fire related. While we were dating, he did have to help with the Numbers Fire that burned over eighteen thousand acres just south of the city. After that, there were many *When I was fighting for my life in the fire* stories. Wildly exaggerated, I'm assuming. He came back without even a scratch on him.

"You seem like the type of man who does what you do," I say. "Running a company, investing in golf courses."

"How so?"

I lift a shoulder and let it drop. "I don't know, you just look the part. Well-polished, put together." I gesture toward him sitting next to me, his stark-white polo stain-free even though we spent the last four hours walking an eighteen-hole course in the outdoors.

I tap my lips with my index finger. "I bet your house is meticulous. Minimal, with very little color. Mostly gray tones." I'm pretty good at this game. Just by talking to someone, it's pretty easy to tell what kind of home they live in.

Aidan gives me a stony glare before taking a drink of his beer. He wipes his lips with the back of his fingers. "You'd be wrong," he says.

"Really?" I tilt my head, not believing him. "I so rarely am."

This makes Aidan's lips pull upward, his teeth peeking through this time. He's got nice ones—teeth, that is. Straight and white. The lips are nice too. He's not one of those big-mouth smile guys, nor does he laugh all that much. At least not since I've known him. But when his lips pull upward, like they are right now, and when he does let out a little chuckle, like I've heard him do a couple of times, I can't deny the fact it makes a little trickle of joy drop into my belly. It's a good feeling. A very *friendly* feeling. There are only *friend* feelings here. Nothing else.

"And I bet you drive" — I twist my lips to the side as I think — "a Mercedes."

Aidan just stares at me. *Aha! I got him.*

"How would you know that?"

I lift a shoulder and let it drop. "You just seem like the type."

"Really?"

"Well, that. And also, I parked next to a sleek-looking one in the fairly empty parking lot when I first got here. So it was an educated guess."

He chuckles, and my belly does a little dance. *Stop it.*

"So, did you not have a choice? With the family business?" I ask him and then take a sip of my drink.

Aidan looks down at his hands, which are now settled on his lap, his fingers intertwined. "Not really," he says.

"Are you unhappy with that?"

"No," he says, looking back at me and shaking his head. "I mean, every once in a while, I wonder . . . but, no. This is my family's legacy, after all. My great-great-grandfather started it."

I nod, remembering the story on the website about the original Jacob St. Claire and how he built the company, pretty much with his bare hands.

I nibble on my bottom lip, wondering if Aidan will want to answer my next question. I decide to take a chance and ask it anyway. "Why did the company go to you and not your older brother?" It seems like in the line of succession, the business would have gone to Jake St. Claire first.

Aidan's jaw does that twitching thing. He clears his throat once. I have instant regrets for asking.

"Never mind," I say, waving the words away with a flip of my hand.

Aidan looks at me. "He couldn't."

I can tell by his look of finality that this is all the answer I will get from him on the subject. This would usually prompt me to ask little questions here and there to see if I can piece it all together, but this feels like none of my business. Or at least business that Aidan doesn't want me to know about.

Something dawns on me then. "Why is your last name St. Claire if that's your mother's family?"

"Good question," he says, bobbing his head. "My mom was the only child my grandparents could have, and so when she married my dad, she kept her name, and for the sake of the family business, it was agreed that my brother and I would take her name."

"Gotcha," I say, nodding my head. That's different — but no stranger than sisters marrying brothers, like in my family. "Did your mom work for the company?"

"She did," he says, his tone and his facial features instantly brighten. "She ran it for a while. But it was never her thing. As soon as I was capable enough, she let me take over."

"How old were you when that happened?"

"Twenty-five," he says.

My eyes widen on their own. "That's a young age to be running a business."

"I have the gray hairs to prove it."

"You do not," I say through a laugh.

He pulls off his cap and runs his hand through his dark hair to straighten it. It's thick and quite pretty. Even so, I absolutely do *not* want to run my own fingers through it.

He turns his head and combs back the sides of his hair with his fingers, and sure enough, if you look closely — which I had to do, by leaning toward him — there are a handful of gray strands.

"Well," I say, pulling my head back. Not noticing at all how he smelled with the close proximity. I definitely did *not* notice the woodsy scent mixed with some sort of citrus. Nor did I care for the aroma. At all.

He insulted your family farm, Jenna! Remember the farm.

That seems to do the trick. I take a large inhale. "There really is some gray," I confirm. "You must hold your age well. How old are you? Forty? Fifty?"

He chuckles. I feel that little dance of joy in my belly. *The farm! The farm!* "I'm thirty-three," he says. I'd already put that together from our first conversation at the Eagle's Den.

Aidan puts his cap back on, thankfully frontward. If he'd done the backward thing again, I think I . . . well, let's all just be grateful he didn't.

"I'm thirty," I say. "I thought I'd just tell you instead of you awkwardly having to ask, since you're not supposed to ask a woman her age."

He nods. "I wasn't going to ask."

"Really? You're not curious at all?" Why does this sting just the teeniest, tiniest bit?

"I didn't need to," he says, in that dry way he talks. "I guessed it already."

"You did not," I exclaim, louder than I meant to. Luckily the large room is fairly empty, save Tom and the couple sitting in front of the stone fireplace on the opposite end.

If there's one thing I have to thank Dana Peterson for, it's her skin. No one has ever guessed that she's fifty-six. If it weren't for her roots that she hasn't dyed in a while, she'd look like she was in her forties. People mostly guess that I'm in my mid-twenties. Josie too.

"I would have guessed twenty-two," he says.

"Now you're just patronizing me."

Aidan smiles, even bigger this time. And dang it all, my stomach does a little flip.

"What about you?" he asks.

"What about me?"

"Is running a farm in your future?"

I shake my head. "No. I'll probably help during pumpkin season until I die. But the day-to-day won't be me."

"Who will run it, then? When your aunt and mom can't anymore?"

"My uncle and dad run it too," I say. "Apparently not all that well, according to someone I met recently."

He looks to the ceiling and then down at me. "Are you ever going to forgive me for that?"

"Probably not." I have to hold on to it, actually. It's crucial to my plan.

Oh crap, *my plan*. We've been talking so easily that I almost forgot why I was here.

"Aidan, we have work to do," I say, taking my phone out from my pocket and pulling up my list.

"What work?"

"To get you ready for your conference," I say.

I look over at him to see him scowling. "I thought we were working on it."

"No," I say. "This is us just chatting. You need to be practicing."

"Practicing?"

"Yes, I did some research and the best way to help you feel more at ease talking to strangers is to practice."

I look at my list. "Okay, so I thought we could do a little role-playing," I tell him.

I look over and see that he's leaned in and has seen the list.

"What are you doing?" I swipe the phone away from him, holding it close to my chest. It annoys me to no end when someone looks at my phone without asking. What if I were looking at nudes or something? Well, I'd never do that. But what if? My phone is my private property.

"Sorry," he says. "The top part caught my eye."

I pull my phone back just a little and look at it and let out a little squeal before giving him a sheepish sort of grin. I can feel heat rising up my neck.

He cocks his head to the side. "Did it say *How to Help Aidan St. Claire Not Be a Jackass*?"

"No," I say, sounding defensive.

"Yes, it did," he says. "I saw it in big black lettering at the top."

Gah. I take a couple of breaths, trying to stall so I can come up with an explanation. I decide on the truth. "I apologize," I start. "However, it was more a response to what you said about the farm."

"Right." He reaches up and rubs his jaw. "May I?" he asks, holding out a hand.

"May you what?"

"I just want to fix something," he says. "I won't touch anything else."

I reluctantly hand him my phone, the list with the big black letters practically screaming from the screen.

He types just a few things and then hands it back to me.

I look down at it, confused. "You removed *jack*," I say.

"I don't want to be compared to a donkey."

"You'd rather be compared to a butt?"

He just shrugs. "I've been called worse."

This makes me snort out a laugh.

"I can change it," I say. "What about *How to Help Aidan St. Claire Not Be a Brick Wall*?"

He smiles this time and does that dang chuckling thing, which I ignore by quickly looking down at my phone and changing the title of my list.

"Okay, so role-playing," I say, setting my phone down on the counter.

"How about we do that another time," Aidan says.

"But that's not why I'm here."

"Yeah, but . . ." He looks around the room. "I think it's been nice just to talk. I don't do this kind of thing often. This is helping me too."

I let out a breath. "Okay, but the next time we meet, we're sticking to my plan."

"Sounds good."

Chapter Twelve

Jenna Peterson's Guide to Dating Emotionally Unavailable Men:

You may find that you will learn more about them through texting or other nonconfrontational ways of communication. A good phone plan and solid Wi-Fi are important.

On Saturday, we finally hit the first day of October, and the pumpkin patch is hopping. Even though we open in September, there's something about the next month that really kicks people into the spirit of the season. We've been so busy I haven't even had a chance to talk to Josie; she's been reading Priscilla Pumpkin stories around the clock with barely a break. At least the donation jar was pretty full today, which will add more time to my end-of-the-day duties. Lots of bills to separate and coins to roll.

This is all good, of course. But it's almost closing time and my feet are killing me. All I want to do right now is go home and curl up with Can Yaman and my Turkish dramas. Instead, I get to go help an introverted man work on some extroverted skills. We decided on tonight after the golfing failure. Which actually wasn't a total failure, I guess. We did talk at the clubhouse afterward, and I did learn some things about Aidan. I suppose that was all a step in the right direction. It was forward momentum. But we don't have time for steps. We need long jumps or pole vaults.

Because of both Aidan's and my schedules, we couldn't make anything work until tonight, and so we're meeting up at another restaurant. And we are going to role-play our hearts out. Which is something I never thought I'd be doing at the age of thirty. Josie and I did a lot of make-believe playing growing up together on this farm. I have no doubt I'll be able to do it.

While we couldn't meet up until tonight, we've filled the gap with a bit of texting. Aidan is actually pretty witty via text. Like some of his walls come down behind a phone. Maybe it's the fact that he can think about things before he texts. I briefly wondered if maybe that was the answer to his problem. He could just text everyone at the conference. *How about you give me your number and we can chat about this via text?* It probably wouldn't work. Certainly not with golfing. And it would make the gala super awkward.

I feel like I saw another side to him, though. Like this exchange we had a couple of nights ago. I was lying in my bed trying to watch the Turkish soap opera Josie and I love so much when my phone dinged.

Aidan: You never answered my question about the farm
Me: What?
Aidan: I asked you after golfing who was going to run it when your parents and aunt and uncle retire
Me: Were you lying in bed and this question popped into your brain?
Aidan: How did you know? Are you watching me?
Me: Educated guess

Me: My cousin Oliver most likely

Aidan: Why him?

Me: Because he wants to

Aidan: And you don't?

Me: The farming life is not for me

Then he sent me a GIF of Judy Garland riding a tractor.

Me: Did you really send me a gif?

Aidan: I did

Me: Why do I find this shocking?

Aidan: Do you pronounce gif with a G or a J?

Me: G, of course. I'm not a monster.

Aidan: Good answer

Me: Or do you mean jood answer?

Aidan: Jood night

I laughed out loud. It was all so unexpected. And it made me want to text him more. Which then made me realize I need to be careful with this guy. I've fallen for a witty, emotionally unavailable man before. I know how that kind of relationship ends. I am not going there again.

I begin the arduous task of counting the donations, and just as I'm stacking all the bills into piles, someone comes in the door. It's my dad, looking like a poster child for farming in a red-and-yellow flannel shirt under a pair of jean overalls and old, worn-out work boots on his feet. He's got some sort of mud stain on one of his knees, which only adds to the vibe.

"Hey, Little Pumpkin," he says.

Okay, I know it's totally cliché for our family to work on a pumpkin farm and for my dad's term of endearment for me to be *pumpkin*, and I'm not exactly little anymore, but I don't care. I love it and I'm keeping it.

"Hey, Dad," I say, giving him a smile. "You done for the day?"

"I'm letting your uncle Charles make the last run," he says.

"Busy day," I say.

"It was," he says. "How do the donations look today?"

I tap on the jar with a fingernail. "Not too shabby."

"Do you think we'll make it?"

"I . . . do." I wouldn't have been able to say that ten days ago. Thanks to Aidan St. Claire, I truly do think we will be able to pull this off.

He runs his fingers through his thinning hair. "Well, I like the confidence. I'm not so sure. Your mom and your aunt have got us all working to come up with ideas. And honestly, I hate the idea of having to ask in the first place."

"Yeah, Mom told me she was looking for ideas. Maybe I'll get back in her good graces by managing to bring in something big," I say. This is my actual hope.

He tilts his head to the side, giving me a curious look. "What makes you think you're not?"

"Well, it all started when I was born . . ."

"Jenna," my dad chides, in that low, comforting tone of his. "You don't have to do anything to prove yourself to your mom or me."

"Sure, sure," I say, not really wanting to get into it right now. I have many deep-seated issues with my mom. I've failed her by not living closer to home, not having settled down or produced any children yet, and not having a *real* job. And probably many, many other things.

"You know she loves you, Jenna."

"I know," I say. And I do know. She just has a strange way of showing it.

As if summoned by our conversation about her, my mom opens the door and walks into the ticket office. Seriously, how does she do it?

"Craig," she says, slightly out of breath, orange beret atop her head. "I'm glad I found you. We need your help with the bunnies."

"What's going on?" my dad asks.

"Oh, that Jezebel of a bunny got into the pen again," she says.

"Jezebel?" my dad and I say at the same time.

She looks to the left like she's trying to think really hard. She turns her gaze back to us. "What's the same sort of thing, but for a male?"

"A gigolo?" I say.

"A pimp?" my dad throws out there.

"A Casanova?" I say.

My dad snaps his fingers toward me. "A Don Juan."

"Oh, good one, dad."

My mom clears her throat loudly. "Thank you so much for that." She turns her body toward my dad. "That *rascal* of a bunny has gotten out of his hutch again and into the pen with all the females and he's been"—she lowers her chin like she's about to tell us something big—"having his way with them." She ekes that last part out in a quiet, almost whispered way, as if she'll get struck down if she says it too loud.

I snort out a laugh, and if her head could do a full 360 swivel before landing on me, it would. "Don't be crass, Jenna," she says. "It's nature's way."

"You won't be saying that when we have hordes of baby bunnies around here," I say.

"So what am I supposed to do about it?" my dad asks. He's had a long day himself, taking trailer loads of folks to the pumpkin patch with his tractor.

"I got him out," she says. "Because there were a bunch of children gathered around when he was found in the pen. And Jonathan was there giving everyone an education on boy parts and girl parts."

"Oh dear," I say, trying hard to hold in my laughter picturing my nephew informing everyone of his knowledge of human anatomy. That must have brought up a lot of questions some parents were not prepared to answer.

"But then he got away from me, and I need you to find him."

My dad's shoulders drop, and he lets out a heavy breath. "Can't we just set the dogs on him?"

"Rufus is our prize-winning buck," she says. "We need him for breeding. Just not in front of the kids, or in an entire pen of does."

"That are probably already knocked up," I say, under my breath. But she heard me. I got the *Dana Peterson flared nostrils of disappointment* look.

"I'm on it," he says, not very enthusiastically and practically dragging himself from the office.

"Jenna," she says to me. "Sit up straight."

"Yes, Mother," I say, a bit robotically.

"I like your makeup today. Very natural."

"I'm not wearing any," I tell her and give her a bright smile.

"Well, then you don't need it." She returns the smile.

And with that, she's out the door. This time of year, when my mom is too busy to have a proper conversation with me, really gives me life. It's like a quick fast-food version of her. Next month she'll be back to her full-five-course-meal nagging ways.

She's wrong about the makeup thing, though. I do need some. At least a little to cover up the bags that will surely start forming under my eyes at any minute. I also need a shower and some clothes that don't smell like I've been at a farm all day.

But first, I have to count a bunch of money.

"You won't even try?" I ask Aidan as we sit across from each other in a booth at the South Shore Café. It's more of an upscale burger joint, with the dim lighting and the brick walls. During the day they have a beautiful outdoor patio seating area with views of the mountains and the lake. It's much more my style than the steak house we were at last Sunday. There's only one fork, one knife, and one spoon, and they are all wrapped in a napkin. Just the way I like it. Although currently, utensils have been cleared off the table and my napkin is balled up next to me on the booth. My belly is nice and full and I've probably got some killer onion breath.

"I'm telling you right now I won't be any good at it," he says.

"You never played pretend when you were growing up?" This is really throwing a wrench in my plans.

"Not really."

"Not even with your . . ." I stop myself before the word *brother* exits my mouth. First of all, I'm not supposed to mention the b-word. It's not an official rule, just one I've gathered. And the other reason is, after doing the math I realized that he and

Jake were seven years apart. That's practically like being raised as an only child. Not close enough in age to be able to have anything in common. By the time Aidan was old enough to play, Jake would have probably been over it. This is all an assumption of course.

"Not even with friends?" I ask instead.

"Maybe, when I was younger; I don't really remember."

"What kinds of things did you do with your friends when you got older?" Even though this has nothing to do with role-playing, or helping him with what he needs, I'm curious about teenage Aidan St. Claire. What was he like in high school? How did this reserved man act back then? Was he like talking to a brick wall then too? Not that I'd call him that myself. His answers may be on the shorter side, but he's never unwilling to answer my questions. Unless they're about his brother.

"Sports, mainly."

"What did you play?" I ask.

"Football and lacrosse."

"Did you play in high school?"

"I did. I played backup quarterback for the first two years and starting my junior and senior."

"You went to Aspen Lake High, right?"

He gives me a nod.

"We're rivals. I went to Carson. I might have cheered at one of your games."

"Maybe," he says.

"Did you like high school?" I ask.

"Yeah, I had some great friends. We had a really solid group. We hung out at each other's houses, went to school dances in groups. That kind of stuff."

Aidan St. Claire at a school dance? This I'd like to see.

"Are you still friends with any of them?"

"We keep in touch, but most of them moved away. My closest friend, Gabe, moved to Reno."

I find this interesting. Not one of my past four boyfriends had anyone they were super close to, mostly just groups they hung out with. I always wondered why that was.

"Did you like it . . . uh, high school?" he asks me.

"Yeah, sure," I say.

High school wasn't all that horrible. Josie had her pirate drama, but that never affected me like it did her. But when I think back on the me that existed in high school—the one who had big future plans—I feel like I disappointed her somehow. High school Jenna had it all figured out. I was going to get my degree, have a fantastic career in public relations, and be married by twenty-five, with a couple of kids by the time I was thirty. And now look at me. Not that my life is bad. Well, maybe the whole only-attracting-difficult-men aspect and not knowing what being in love is like aren't so great. It just goes to show, you can't plan out your life.

"Are you still close with Gabe?" I ask Aidan.

He gives me a sort of irritated look when I ask him this, and I wonder if I've touched on a subject akin to his brother. Which is confusing since he brought it up first. But then he relaxes his face. "We talk often. But he's married and has two kids. So our lives are pretty different now."

"Right. You're the big-time CEO." I give him a teasing grin.

His lips pull upward, slightly. "I guess. But I'd like that life someday—the one Gabe has."

"Married with kids?"

He dips his chin, just once, his eyes on mine. I don't want to picture it, but I can't help myself. Aidan holding a tiny baby with those sexy forearms of his, his lips pulled upward as he stares at the bundle. There's something about a man holding a baby that's so attractive. Even Reginald the Pretentious seemed less full of himself when he'd hold my niece and nephews as newborns.

I clear my throat because I'm taking us off on a tangent here and also because I need to stop this train of thought for myself. Aidan will meet a woman someday, fall in love, get married, and have a baby with her. And that woman will probably be the person he meets just after spending time with me. Why does that thought bother me? *Because you have a type, Jenna, and you are trying to change that, remember?*

"So, back to role-playing," I say.

"Do we have to?" he asks. He looks around the room. "It's crowded in here."

"No one's paying attention to us," I say adamantly. "How are you going to talk to people at the conference? It'll be crowded there, you know. You can't one-word answer your way through it."

"I haven't been giving you one-word answers today."

"That's true. But I'm not some random stranger. I'm like a less random stranger."

This gets me a small smile.

"Come on," I say.

He lets out a frustrated-sounding breath through his teeth. "Fine, let's try it."

I smile. "Okay." I rub my hands together. "So, we are going to act like I've approached you at your booth at the conference."

"Okay," he says, skeptically.

"You will be playing the part of yourself. Shouldn't be too hard, yes?"

He scowls at me.

"Just humor me, okay?"

"Go ahead." He holds his hand out to me, palm up, like he's giving me the stage. Which I take and plan to knock his socks off. Since I've come prepared.

I clear my throat. "Hello," I say, holding out a hand to shake Aidan's. He reluctantly gives me his.

"Hi," he says back. No inflection in his tone. Nothing indicating he's meeting a potential customer here.

I let out a harrumph and drop my shoulders. "This is important, remember? Can you try, just a little?"

He sits up straight. "All right," he says. "Hello, can I help you?"

"I'm Kim Russell from Barnes Creek Industries. I'd love to talk to you more about putting some of our boats in your store."

Aidan pulls his chin inward, looking at me as if I have two heads. "How do you know about Barnes Creek Industries?"

"My family owns it," I say, staying in character, giving him my best cheesy grin. I'm mentally taking notes on what he's doing wrong here, which is all the things. All of it.

"Wait, did you research boat manufacturers?" he asks me.

"Aidan," I say, dropping my character, my voice chastising. "You're not even trying."

He chuckles. "You put a lot of work into this, didn't you?"

I lean back and fold my arms. "Of course," I say, and then look to the side, feeling sort of foolish for doing that—for investing all the time that I did. Like maybe I tried too hard and should have just come up with a fake name off the cuff. "You asked me to help. And you're paying me a lot of money to do it. I wanted this to be as authentic as possible."

"How did you find this particular company?"

I shrug one shoulder. "Google, of course. I found a list of the top boat manufacturers in the country and picked one with a female owner. Do you know that quite a few of the companies on that list are from Louisiana?"

"I did know that," he says. "Barnes Creek is one of the top sailboat makers."

I smile. "That's right." I happened to pick it because I know Aidan likes to go sailing. A little sucking up to the boss, I suppose.

"I know them well," Aidan says.

"Then this whole role-playing thing shouldn't be a stretch for you." I fold my arms, giving him what I hope is a very pouty face.

"This is true. But maybe I should tell you that Kim Russell is a very nice *man*," he says.

I feel instant heat on my face. "Right," I say, keeping as straight of a face as possible. It's not easy. I clear my throat, hold out my hand, and in the deepest manly voice I can muster, I say, "Hello, Aidan, I'm Kim Russell from Barnes Creek Industries."

Then Aidan does something I've yet to see him do. He throws back his head and lets out a laugh. It's a full-blown guffaw. It's frustratingly charming the way his mouth goes wide, his perfect teeth in full view. I'm not sure how to handle this. His chuckle makes my stomach flip. This laugh . . . well, it has a whole-body effect on me.

Aidan can't seem to stop himself. He's even pulled the napkin off his lap and is now dabbing his eyes. I've been twisting my lips to the side, trying not to give him the satisfaction, but once he does the eye dabbing thing, I can't help myself and I start laughing too.

"You're ruining my role-playing," I say to him once we've both calmed down and are only chuckling a little now.

"Sorry," he says, smiling. "I haven't laughed like that in a long time."

"Yes, and at my expense," I say. I meant it to be more annoyed sounding, but I'm still grinning, so it doesn't have the same effect.

"Should we try again?"

"No," I say.

He gives me a very promising—albeit mostly fake—expression. With his lips doing a twitching thing like he wants to laugh again. "I promise I'll try harder."

"It's not that." I look around the room, at the people sitting in booths on either side of us and tables full of people in the open space, and decide that this isn't going to work, not here at least. "I think we need a better setting to do this in. What are you doing next week?"

Chapter Thirteen

Jenna Peterson's Guide to Dating Emotionally Unavailable Men:

Asking for a commitment will be like trying to get blood from a stone. Expect excuses.

"That feels great," Evie, one of my regulars at the spa, says as I lightly massage her shoulders, working my way up to her neck. She's got a cooling masque on her face and cotton pads on her eyes.

It's Monday and we're in one of the three facial rooms we have at the spa. My least favorite one because it's got the smallest amount of space and I've already hit my hip on the counter more than once and there'll definitely be a bruise there, under my scrubs that offer little protection. I had to curse in my head so I didn't disturb the client, and it was definitely a word that would make the sisters faint and probably try to exorcise a demon out of me.

Because the spa is attached to one of the more luxurious hotels in the town, I mostly get out-of-towners in for services. But there are a handful of locals who frequent the spa, which makes it more fun. Especially the kind that love to fill me in on town gossip. And Evie knows everything about everyone in

Aspen Lake. She's been around this town for a while and gives me the scoop on her sister, Nicolette, who happens to be Reece the Pirate's ex-wife. She's a real piece of work, that one. I hope Josie never has a run-in with her. I can't imagine she'll be able to avoid it, though — not with how close they seem to be getting. I've hardly spoken to Josie in the last week. Except for a few texts and quick hellos at the farm. Yesterday was so busy, she was only able to wave at me as she walked past the ticketing booth.

I hear a lot of stories when I'm in the facial rooms. There's something about lying in this bed with the quiet new age music, the smell of essential oils filling the space. People tend to talk. A lot. I barely have to use any of my questioning skills. They just spill. I've heard some of the deepest, darkest secrets in this room. Nothing illegal yet. But Chantelle once had a guy — a guest at the hotel — who told her about how he might be going to jail for murder. That one was a little crazy. And a lot scary.

Some people don't want to talk when they come in, and that's okay too. You can usually tell within the first few minutes if you've got a talker or not. Evie is definitely a talker.

"Anyway," Evie says. "I just can't help wonder if Nicolette hadn't gotten caught up with that St. Claire loser, maybe things would have been different."

I take in a quick inhale and stop massaging, my fingers still lingering at the base of her neck. "Did you say St. Claire?"

"Yeah, have you heard of him?" she asks. "Terrible person. His family owns that boating company on Lake Boulevard. I'm pretty sure his name is Jake."

My stomach does a little bobbing thing. Up and down. Upset and then relief. Not that I thought Aidan was who Evie was talking about. I mean, I did, but only for like half a second. Also, why would it bother me if it were Aidan?

"I know his brother," I say, and then start working on her neck again.

"Oh yes, Aidan St. Claire?"

"Yes," I confirm.

"He's not much better from what I've heard."

There goes my stomach sinking again. Even though my head is already presenting arguments. I certainly don't have any evidence.

"What have you heard?" I can't help asking.

"Not that he's a partier. But I've heard he's a player. One of those eternal bachelors."

That doesn't match with the conversation we had last night. But it does work well with the emotional unavailability I pegged him for from the beginning. None of this should bother me, though. So why does it? Probably because it doesn't ring true. Or maybe because I don't want it to be true. I think I'm just going to stop this whole thought train from leaving the station.

"Their family has been around for ages," she keeps going. "I've heard Jake St. Claire hasn't been seen or heard from in years."

"Right," I say, giving her a simple one-word reply. Maybe she'll move on.

"I also heard that Jake was supposed to run the family business—that boating company," she says. She's not going to move on, but I'm suddenly back to being curious again.

"What happened?" I ask.

"I heard he couldn't make it through rehab or something."

"Wow," I say. If that's true, it fits well into the puzzle. I don't know the whole story, of course. And I try to take everything Evie says with a grain of salt. But it does explain a lot — possibly why Aidan doesn't want to talk about his brother, and why there might be animosity between the two of them.

Regardless, I feel like I should shut this conversation down. If this is true, then Aidan's relationship with his brother is more complex than the big fight I had pegged to be the cause of the rift between them. This isn't Evie's story to tell.

She lets out a breath. "That sister of mine . . ."

"You know," I jump in before she can continue, "I forgot to tell you. We just got this lovely lip masque in. It makes your lips feel full and soft. Do you want to try it?"

"Oh, that sounds nice."

This is usually an upsell, but today it's on the house.

"You'll love it," I tell her. "You just have to keep your mouth very still."

"I'm sorry, I don't know anyone named Josie," I say into my phone as I sit in the break room at work.

"I'm sorry," Josie says, her voice pitch going up as she draws out the words. It's a very whining sound.

My phone vibrated in my pocket as soon as I finished with a client and entered the little room at the back the building where some days I spend the bulk of my time, especially when we're slow. Today is not one of those days. I still have three more treatments to go.

"It's fine," I tell her. And it really is. I'm just giving her crap. But I do miss her. "How goes the pirate life?" I ask her.

"It's definitely for me," she says through a laugh. "What's new with you?"

"Same old, same old," I say. Lying through my teeth. My life is quite different lately. Because of a certain man that I won't be telling Josie about. Not now, at least. It's much too long of a conversation. "Are you talking to your mom yet?" I ask to change the subject.

Josie recently had a talk with her mom regarding Reece. It didn't go well. But there were things that needed to be said, and hopefully over time their relationship will heal.

"Not really," she says on a sigh. "She's still avoiding me."

"I need to call my mom to the curb so she can avoid me too," I say.

"You really should — it's been kind of nice."

"It's a wonder we turned out normal with the sisters around."

She snorts into the phone. "Uh, we didn't."

"Good point," I say, and we both laugh.

"I miss you," she says.

"Me too, Jo Jo. I feel like I haven't seen you in forever," I say, my voice sounding as whiny as hers did.

"I know. As soon as I get through the school carnival this weekend, we're hanging out, okay?"

"I'm holding you to that."

"Gotta run," she says, talking fast. "I just wanted to hear your voice. But now I need to get back to my class."

I wish she didn't have to hang up, but I'm also relieved. I'm afraid I might start spilling everything about Aidan to Josie if we keep talking, and I'm not ready to tell her. I haven't told anyone about him, especially not my family. That's because it's a strange situation, and I don't want anyone to get their hopes up about the money because there's no guarantees with that. No contract was signed, and Aidan and I haven't made much headway there anyway. I don't think I've helped him at all. I know he said he'd pay either way, but that doesn't seem fair to me.

Josie also knows my past history with men and dating. All the gory details. Aidan St. Claire is exactly the kind of man I need to keep at arm's length. I don't want Josie to read more into the situation and worry that I'm getting sucked into the same trap. I'm not, and I don't need her worrying about it or checking up on me.

"My feet are killing me," Chantelle declares as she enters the break room, Heather following behind her, both taking seats at the white, round table. "This was not a good day for Chantelle to break in new shoes."

"Always a bad idea on a busy day," I say. After Evie, I had another facial with someone staying at the lodge, and then a regular client who comes in for microdermabrasion. This is the first break I've had all day.

"No kidding," she says.

My phone vibrates, rattling the table, and the screen lights up with Aidan St. Claire's name in a green box.

"Isn't that the guy with the fifty dollars?" Heather asks, pointing at my phone.

Crap. I pick it up and hold it to my chest, looking like a toddler who's trying to hide the treat they weren't supposed to eat. I just declared myself guilty.

I know what the text is probably about. We're supposed to be meeting tonight, and he's probably confirming.

"The one that insulted your family farm?" Chantelle pipes in.

"Why are you talking to him?" Heather asks.

"I'm . . . not," I say by way of denial. It's not a lie, per se. I received a text from him, not a call. We've never actually spoken on the phone, except for the first time when I told him about the money.

They both stare at me. "Fine, he apologized," I say.

"So what, are you now like besties or something?" Chantelle asks, giving me a confused look.

"No, not like that," I say.

"What is it, then?" Heather asks, her brow furrowed.

"Ooooh, I see what's going on here. You're dating," Chantelle says, bobbing her head up and down like she just figured out all the world's mysteries.

"No," I say adamantly. "We're friends, sort of. It's complicated."

Chantelle's eyebrows move up her head. "You always give me that excuse."

I pull my chin inward, giving myself double or possibly triple chins. "No I don't."

"Yes, you do; anytime you don't want to tell me the whole story, you say, 'It's complicated.'" She imitates me but with a more goofy-sounding voice.

I scrunch my face at her, my mind working through what she's saying. It's a phrase everyone has said at some point. But it's not something I *always* say. I'm an open book most of the time.

"Spill it," Chantelle says, her eyes wide, her lips pulled into an almost pucker.

I let out a breath. "He's asked me to help him with something," I say.

"Like what? Getting out of his pants?" Chantelle says.

"N—no," I stammer, giving her an awkward laugh. "It's a project, for his work."

"That's a little too vague," Heather says.

"It's . . ."

"Complicated?" Chantelle cuts me off.

"No," I say, feeling more and more annoyed. "I was going to say it's hard to explain."

"That's another way of saying it's complicated," she says. "And don't try to come back at me with 'It's a long story' either. Same thing."

"I love long stories," Mr. Hot Doctor says, waltzing into the break room in dark scrubs and a white coat with the spa name embroidered on the pocket.

I've never been happier to have him interrupt a conversation, which is his MO.

"Yes, and I'm sure you also enjoy long walks on the beach and dancing in the rain," Chantelle says, straight faced.

"Of course," he says, smiling that bright smile of his at the three of us and taking a seat at the only empty chair between Heather and me. "What can I say? I'm a romantic at heart."

I don't think he caught on to Chantelle's joke.

"I bet you are," she says, her dark-brown eyes moving briefly up to the ceiling.

"How's everyone's day going?" he asks, leaning back in his chair, his large hands resting atop his thighs.

"Great," Heather says. "But I've got to get ready for a client." She bobs a head over at the clock on the wall.

I still have another ten minutes before I need to set up for mine.

"Oh shoot," Chantelle says, her lips pulled downward and her eyebrows moving upward. "I'm going to be late for mine." She points a finger at me. "We're not done here."

I just give her a placating look. Or maybe it ended up being more resigned because I know Chantelle, and she won't let this go.

"What did I miss?" Mr. Hot Doctor asks as the other two hurry out the door. "What was the long story?"

"Nothing," I say, waving a hand at him and shaking my head. "Just girl talk."

"I love girl talk," he says, giving me a charming smile. Or at least I think that's what he's going for. It's bordering on smarmy.

"You do?"

"Oh sure. Try me," he says. "Tell Dr. Shackwell what's going on."

Shackwell! I knew it started with an *S-h*. Also, it's cute when Chantelle refers to herself in the third person, but this guy? Not so much.

"Is it boy problems?" He leans in toward me, giving me a version of Josie's teacher face, but it just comes off as smooth and practiced . . . in a bad way.

I know this game all too well. Mr. Hot Doctor—or Dr. Shackwell—is the textbook definition of emotionally unavailable. He's fishing to find out if I'm dating someone. If he were emotionally sound, he would just outright ask.

"Yes," I say. "I've been dating a man. For a while now. I think it's time we settled down. How long do you think a couple should date before getting married?"

Ah, yes. The m-word. That's the best way to put people like Dr. Shackwell off. Just the thought of the institution probably makes him twitchy. His face actually fell when I said it.

"Um, . . . I . . . That's a good question," he says, practically stumbling over his words. "I guess it depends on the relationship. There really isn't a set time for these things."

I wish I would have written down what I predicted his response would be. Because that was pretty much it. And oh my gosh, is that a bead of sweat on his forehead?

"How long do you think?" I place my elbow on the table and lean into it, my chin resting on my fist.

"Oh, I don't know," he says, his eyes darting around the room. "Like maybe four years . . . or ten?"

Nailed it.

I let out a breath and sit back in my chair, and then I reach over and place a hand on his arm to offer him comfort, because I sort of feel sad that something happened in his life to make him the way he is—so scared of being open.

"Dr. Shackwell." I give him a serious look. "I don't know you all that well. But I see a man who doesn't know how to truly be himself around people. I see someone who's hiding behind a façade. And I hope someday you figure all that out so you can find a meaningful relationship. One you feel comfortable in, and with someone you'll want to share everything about yourself with."

He just stares at me.

"You deserve better."

He looks at me for a few more beats, and then he quickly looks down at his watch. "Oh shoot," he says and then rolls his lips together while nodding his head. "I've got a client coming in. It was great talking to you." He stands up and is out the door so quickly, it's almost cartoonish. Like if I looked closely enough there'd be a ghostly imprint of him left there, hanging under the doorframe.

Chapter Fourteen

Jenna Peterson's Guide to Dating Emotionally Unavailable Men:

Their home will reflect who they are. Don't be surprised if it's utterly lacking in warmth or originality.

Later that night, after entering the gate code Aidan had sent me earlier, I pull into the driveway of his modern mountain home. It was so far up the mountain, I'd joked to myself that maybe I should have brought some oxygen with me just in case there wasn't enough up here.

The house from the outside looks to be sizeable—but not overly so. It definitely exudes wealth. And it's all in shades of gray. The entire place—at least on the outside—is just as I thought, just as I predicted. *You've still got it, Jenna.*

I park on the large driveway in front of the house and get out. I take in a big gulp of the cold, fresh mountain air, and it's glorious and plentiful. No extra oxygen needed. Not that I was actually concerned.

I'm reminded how much I love it up here as I look up and see bright, twinkling stars. They're much dimmer down in the city.

Even with all the gray, it's a beautiful house, for sure, with the angled three-car garage and the stone and wood siding. I can see the beginning of a porch that I bet wraps around the entire back side of the house and probably has gorgeous views of the lake.

I walk up to a large iron door with four semi-opaque glass window cutouts. I take in another big inhale of the crisp night air before ringing the doorbell and soon, through the windows, I can make out a dark form walking toward me.

"Hello," Aidan says after opening the door, his tone sounding like this is a formal meeting but his clothing suggesting otherwise.

He's in a navy-blue V-neck sweater and jeans, and his feet are bare. It suddenly feels kind of intimate to be here with Aidan, at his house, with his naked feet. He also smells good, like he just sprayed himself with that cologne he uses — woodsy paired with a dash of citrus.

A tingle of discomfort mixed with a dose of anxiety moves down my spine. I reach up and touch the gold ring on my necklace. *Get me out of this, Grandma P.*

I'd thought this was a good idea — meeting Aidan on his turf and not in a busy restaurant — so we could try more role-playing in a place where he feels comfortable. But now it feels like a stupid idea. Aidan is a rich man who lives in a big house, and I'm a lowly farm girl asking him to play pretend for the evening.

"Hey there," I say, my voice sounding small, even though it echoes through the large entryway, sporting what I'm guessing are marble floors. They're polished and shining under the canned ceiling lighting, which brightens up the space. As I'd guessed, it's mostly white and gray, save one picture on the wall just inside the door that's a modern-style painting in the colors of navy blue, gray, and a little bit of gold. Interesting . . .

"Come on in," Aidan says. I could be projecting here, but his voice sounds a little forced, like he's feeling anxious too. Even if it's not true, I'm going to hold on to that, because it makes me relax a little.

I slip off my black boots as soon as I walk inside and set them by the door, leaving on the white socks with the bunnies on them. Aidan helps me take off my jacket and tucks it under his arm as he motions for me to follow him.

"Beautiful house," I say as I follow him down the hall. It smells like newer construction, or at least the remnants of it, which makes me wonder how long he's lived here.

"Thank you," he says.

"When did you move in?"

"The build-out was finished around a year ago."

I love the smell of newness — new paint, new wood. It's just so refreshing. All the buildings on the farm smell old . . . because they are. Don't get me wrong, I love that too; there's comfort in knowing what a place will smell like because it's been that way your whole life. Like Josie's house — it always smells like cinnamon because every fall her mom gets one of those cinnamon brooms, and remnants of the scent will stay through the rest of the year. My mom is into all those fancy plug-ins and tends to go for that smell like fresh laundry from the dryer.

I follow him through the large entryway, and we pass an opening on the left where there's a little sitting room and a black baby grand in the corner. Throw pillows, blankets, artwork, and other decor are thoughtfully placed around the room, matching the colors of the modern painting I'd first noticed.

"I like the color," I say, giving credit where credit is due. I was wrong about Aidan, I guess. I mean, there's still a lot of gray in here, but the accents are a surprise. It was probably done by a decorator, but still, it's not what I had expected.

Aidan doesn't say anything. I didn't expect him to gloat because that doesn't seem like him, but I figured I was due at least one smart comment about how I was wrong.

We pass a room with an open barn-style door and I briefly look in to see it's an office. I can't see much because the lights are off, but it appears to be sparse and meticulous—not a scrap of paper on the large desk sitting in the center, a wall of windows behind it. At least I pegged that one. Not like it was hard—you can tell all that just from looking at the guy.

Past the office, the hallway leads into a large space with a living room to the left with tall, vaulted ceilings, and to the right a kitchen with dark-gray cabinets and bright white countertops. All with beautiful hardwood floors throughout, except for the marble in the front entryway.

In the living room, there's an expensive-looking gray leather couch set, which faces a floor-to-ceiling gray stone fireplace and a giant flat-screen television mounted over a wooden mantelpiece.

And there's more color. More in the modern art on the walls, in the throw blankets and the pillows on the couches. There's some color in the throw rug that sits under the large gray-stained wooden coffee table. There are also bowls and a few thoughtfully placed vases around the space making the room feel warm and inviting.

"Would you like a drink?" Aidan asks after opening a small closet and hanging up my coat.

"Sure," I say as I look around, my hands in the back pockets of my jeans. "Some water would be great."

"Be right back. Have a seat," he says with a chin lift toward the larger couch of the set, the one that faces the fireplace.

I take a seat in the corner near the wall. The couch doesn't look like it would be comfortable at all—not like the pretty, inviting pink one at my place—but when you sit down it's much deeper than it looks, and it has just the perfect amount of cushion. I think I could live on this couch the rest of my days, and I might have to. I don't know how I'll get out of it. I pull one of the blue-and-white striped accent pillows from the couch onto my lap, curling my feet up under me.

I like it here. I like being in Aidan's house. Which is a stark contrast to how I felt when I first got here. I reach up and touch the ring hanging around my neck. I guess Grandma P. doesn't need to get me out of this one. Not yet at least.

Something stabs me in the hand as I settle the pillow on my lap, and I turn it over to see one of those heavy cardstock price tags on the back. The kind with the perforated edge that's supposed to be ripped off.

Oh my gosh. Is this new? I look around the room. Is all of this new? He didn't buy all this decor before I got here, did he? No, that's ridiculous. I shake my head at myself. Of course he didn't do that. No one would go to all the trouble.

I can't help myself, though. I give Aidan a smug smile when I hold up the pillow to show him as he walks into the living room from the kitchen, carrying two glasses of water.

"You left a tag," I say, raising my eyebrows as I wait for his reaction.

He doesn't say anything. He sets the drinks down on the coffee table—on coasters of course—and snatches the pillow out of my hand.

"I've had that pillow for years," he says as he rips the tag off, the sound echoing through the room. He shoves it into his pocket and then tosses the pillow on the couch.

I cock my head to the side. "Aidan St. Claire, did you decorate your place just to prove me wrong?"

He scrunches his face at me. "Of course not," he says.

He's lying and he's terrible at it. I can tell by the way he's fidgeting as he sits down on the opposite side of the couch from me. Like he can't get comfortable. As if my finding that price tag made him twitchy. The thing that really gives him away is the redness on the tips of his ears that's working its way up his neck.

I want to laugh and tell him how ridiculous it is. But also, I don't. If it's true—and I'm pretty sure it is—it's sweet, and sort of endearing. Maybe Aidan didn't want to be pegged as a guy who decorated with all gray. Maybe he didn't want me to think that about him. The question is . . . why? It seems like something you'd do to impress someone, like a girlfriend or something. And except for the odd glance here and there, he's given me no indication that he's interested in me, or even attracted to me. Is it a pride thing? He doesn't like the idea of someone calling him out?

What a fascinating man Aidan St. Claire is.

"So," I say, and then sniffle for no reason.

He clears his throat. It's our old standby. The soundtrack to this . . . whatever it is. Working relationship? Friendship?

"Are you ready to do some role-playing?" I ask. "It's serious business this time."

He grumbles out an "I guess."

"I need you to channel your inner child," I say extra dramatically, purposefully being silly to try and lighten his mood so he'll want to do this with me.

"I don't think I have one of those," he says, grumpily.

Clearly. "How did you make it through childhood without playing make-believe?" I ask, remembering our conversation from the other night at the burger restaurant.

"I'm sure I did; I just don't remember it," he says. "I must have grown out of it fast."

One part of my brain—the inquisitive part—wants me to ask him why. The other part—the practical part—wants me to do the job I came here to do.

"Why?" I ask him. My questioning brain won. It almost always does.

Many times my practical brain will say something like: *Maybe you should do your laundry right now, Jenna. You're on your last pair of underwear.* And the other part, the more inquisitive part, will say: *Or . . . you could watch the entire first season of* Ted Lasso.

No regrets. It's a great show.

"I don't know," Aidan says, looking away from me. "It was probably after my dad left."

Oh. Right.

"When you were ten?"

He nods, just once, still looking away.

"Do you ever talk to him?"

He clears his throat. "Every once in a while. He tried to establish a relationship when I got older, but it was too late for that."

I think about my dad and how important he is to me, and how I'd have felt if he'd left. It would have been . . . well, I don't really want to think about that.

"So what happened? Did you feel like you had to grow up when he left?"

His eyes come back to mine, the crystal blue shining in the overhead lighting, his lips pulled slightly downward. "That's exactly how I felt."

"What made you feel that way?" I ask him.

He lifts his shoulders and then drops them as his gaze moves to the coffee table in front of us. "I guess I thought it was my job," he says. I think that's all I'll get from him, but then he continues. "My mom . . . she didn't handle it well, the divorce and my dad just leaving like that. She sort of fell apart. And Jake . . ." He doesn't finish.

I don't press him. I can fill in the blanks with what Evie told me. Aidan took on the responsibility of taking care of everyone, and Jake coped by escaping. And maybe he still does. I'd guess that Aidan is still feeling the responsibility, all these years later. It's why he's running the family business instead of being a teacher, it's why he's fiercely independent, it's why he shows so little emotion. He had to be that way.

I know I probably shouldn't—and my practical brain is telling me not to—but I want to hug him. It's not out of pity or anything like that. It's more a show of understanding—that I get him. I make a snap decision and start to scoot my way down this large couch to where Aidan's sitting on the other end.

"What are you doing?" he asks me, his brows pulled inward.

"I'm going to give you a hug," I say, slightly out of breath. This couch really is massive. I really should have gotten up and walked to him. But in my head, this was the better option.

He gives me that look he often gives me—the one where I have two heads. It's become a thing between us. "Why?" he asks.

"Because I want to," I say, finally reaching him. Before I can second-guess myself or chicken out, I maneuver an arm behind his neck and over his broad shoulders, my other one reaching around the front of him so that my hands meet on the other side. It's a side hug, really. Then I lay my head on his muscular shoulder.

At first, it's like hugging a statue and I wonder if this was a bad idea. Aidan doesn't come off as a hugger, but he also didn't seem horrified when I told him what I was going to do. If he had, I wouldn't have done it. I'm just about to let go because it's feeling extra awkward, but then he starts to relax, and he reaches up and wraps both hands around the arm draped around his front. Then I feel his head lean against mine.

It feels nice. Comfortable, even. I close my eyes and slowly count to ten. I read once that a ten-second hug can actually produce oxytocin. I don't know if it's accurate, but ever since then I've tried to make sure my hugs with my family and close friends were longer. If I can provide the world with more stress-relieving hormones by hugging, then I will.

When I finally get to ten, I'm kind of sad. It went by too fast. But I nudge my head so Aidan lifts his. Then I untangle my hands and sit back a little.

He looks over at me and gives me a closed-mouth smile. "Thank you," he says, laying a hand on my knee and giving it a squeeze. For some reason this feels more intimate than the hug I just gave him.

I sniffle and then move to stand up—which isn't easy; lots of ab muscles are used—Aidan's hand falling away when I do.

"It's time," I say, holding out a hand in front of him.

He lets out a frustrated breath.

"Come on," I say, wiggling the fingers of my outstretched hand at him.

He holds out his hand, and I grab it and tug on him until he's off the couch and standing.

I drag him with me to the kitchen and around the large island in the center of the room. It's a gorgeous space. I'm not all that great of a cook, and I've never been one of those people who have a dream kitchen in their mind. But honestly, if I did have a vision of what I wanted, this would probably be it.

The sisters would swoon if they saw it. My mom would ooh and ahh, and then she'd whip us up something from whatever Aidan had on hand, like the witch that she might possibly be. Seriously, the woman is amazing at making something from nothing. Which is kind of her motto. Something from nothing. Mountains out of molehills. That's my mom and her sister in a nutshell.

"Okay," I say, leaving Aidan on that side of the counter and moving around to the other side.

"What are you doing?" he asks.

"This is our makeshift booth," I tell him. "On that side, where you are, is the booth for Aspen Lake Boating Company. And I will be on this side, as your potential customer."

Aidan lets out a resigned breath, and a muscle twitches in his neck. "You're really going to make me do this?"

"Do you have any other bright ideas?" I ask him.

He runs a few fingers through his hair, messing it up. I push away thoughts of wanting to fix it. *Stop it, brain.*

I move away from the counter and over to the side and then act as if I'm going to walk by, but then stop and turn toward him. Like his booth has caught my attention.

"Oh hey," I say, in a spot-on Memphis accent. I looked it up last night when I was home, sitting on my pink couch. I found a YouTube tutorial on how to do one and picked it up rather fast, if I do say so myself.

I came up with a whole persona. A fake company and employee names. I know exactly what we make, how we make it, and how long it takes. Needless to say, it was probably more research than was necessary. But I wanted this to feel legitimate.

I hold out a hand toward a very reluctant Aidan. "I'm Naomi Baker from Memphis Boatworks."

Aidan looks at my outstretched hand and then looks to the side, pulling his lips between his teeth. So help me if he laughs again . . .

And he does. It's just like the other night. He throws his head back and just lets it out. Loud and boisterous and stupidly adorable.

I hate him right now. Or really, I *want* to hate him. That laugh of his is contagious, and even though I don't want to give him the satisfaction of laughing too, I can't help myself.

"What did I do now?" I finally say, once we're both able to stop, at least for the most part.

Aidan wipes his eyes. "That was the worst southern accent I've ever heard."

"What?" I say through a laugh. "I worked really hard on that."

This makes him start laughing again, the bright noise echoing through the house.

"I think we're going to have to find another way," Aidan says when he's done, wiping at his eyes again.

"Obviously," I say. I should have realized on Saturday night this would never work; then maybe I wouldn't have wasted a whole night doing research. I could have been watching Can Yaman.

Still . . . I don't want to say it was worth it to hear Aidan laugh like he did. But a part of me thinks that maybe it was. Maybe.

"I'm sorry," he says.

"It's fine." I give him a small smile. "I just . . . I just don't want to waste your time."

He looks at me, that serious expression back on his face. "I don't feel like any of this has been a waste of time."

Tiny little silvery butterflies start to move around in my belly with that comment. I ignore them.

"That's good," I say. "At least you've gotten a lot of laughter at my expense." I give him a fake pouting face. I'm not annoyed by it, though. I feel sort of flattered I'm responsible for that laugh of his.

"I can't remember the last time I've laughed that hard," he says.

"Well, at least there's that," I say. I lean my elbows on the counter, resting my chin in my hands. "What am I going to do with you?"

He gives me another one of his serious looks. Those are the kind of looks I expect from Aidan St. Claire—the ones I'm most used to. The smiling and laughing version of Aidan is like a whole other person.

"Honestly," he says. "You've helped me already. More than you could possibly know."

"Whatever," I say, not believing him.

"I'm serious. And if this is too much for you—"

"Oh, no, I'm not giving up," I cut him off. He's not getting away from me that easily. "I'll just have to think of a better plan."

"Okay," he says, his lips pulling upward.

What that plan will be, I have no idea.

Chapter Fifteen

Jenna Peterson's Guide to Dating Emotionally Unavailable Men:

When attempting to offer help, you will get resistance.
Persistence is key.

I do come up with something, and it's good. It's perfect, actually.

I realized it that night after I left Aidan's house, just as I'd gotten into bed and my head hit the pillow—the time that, for normal brains, means sleep. But my brain thinks it's the time to try to solve all the world's problems.

I realized I've been going about this the wrong way all along. I should have recognized it before, but it really hit home when I thought about the decor around Aidan's house and the way he reacted when I showed him the pillow with the tag. Aidan St. Claire is terrible at lying.

So for him, trying to act something out, trying to role-play—that will never work because it's not authentic.

The answer is to put him in real-world situations. And it doesn't have to be related to work, because Aidan has been working for the company since he was fourteen. He knows the insides and outsides of it. It's not like he needs help with that—

he just needs help with feeling more comfortable with himself around people. So that's what we're going to do.

My plan has three parts, and the first part is today. It's a chilly Thursday morning, and I don't have to be to work until two. I've been putting off a bunch of errands in Carson City, so I've made Aidan take the morning off and I've been dragging him around with me. Each place we stop, I give him a challenge—a way for him to work on being chattier. Maybe a question to ask, or a comment to offer. Something to start up a conversation.

To say he isn't thrilled is an understatement.

"I hate this," he says, his face in the same scowl it's been in all morning, as we walk into the beauty-supply place so I can grab some of my favorite shampoo. One benefit of being an aesthetician: I have a beauty license, so I'm able to get all my products at nearly half the regular cost.

The door makes an electronic dinging sound as we enter, and the mostly floral scent from all the shampoo brands, with a dash of nail polish aroma, accosts my nose upon entry.

"What are we doing here again?" Aidan asks, an annoyed look on his face.

"I've already told you. I need some shampoo. And your task," I say, with a bob of my head toward the front counter where a woman with purple hair is scanning items into her computer, "is to ask her to help you find some product for your hair."

"I don't need any product," he says.

I tilt my head to the side. "How do you know that? Maybe she'll show you something you need. Besides"—I reach up and brush some lint from his light-gray jacket with the standing collar, his sleeves pushed up to display his defined forearms—

"you're only here to talk to a real person and ask them questions."

He sighs, and then, putting a hand in the pocket of his jeans, walks over to the checkout counter.

I find the aisle with the brand of shampoo I like, grateful for the low shelving so I can keep an eye on my apprentice and his assignment.

"Hello," I hear him say, in that now-familiar low, gruff tone of his.

"Hi," the woman behind the counter says. "Can I help you find something?" Her voice is higher pitched and a tad nasally. She's smiling at him, her customer service skills on full display.

"Uh . . . yeah," he says. "I was hoping you could help me find some . . . uh, product."

"Of course," she says, extra cheerily. "What exactly are you looking for?"

"Um . . ." I watch as Aidan looks around the room for an answer to this question. In hindsight, maybe I should have given him a little more information with this one.

In my defense, he passed the first test with flying colors. We'd stopped at a local coffee shop that I've missed since moving to Aspen Lake. His assignment was to chat with the barista. To maybe ask him how his day was going.

And it was good. Aidan asked him about his day; the barista — a skinny blond man, probably in his early twenties — was an oversharer, which was perfect. He told him about his day and then asked Aidan about his, and it was a quick little back-and-forth discussion.

I'd been at the other end of the counter waiting for our drinks, watching Aidan chitchat while paying for them.

"Well done," I'd said when he approached me afterward.

He'd let out a breath. "That wasn't so bad."

"Do you really never talk to people when you order food?"

"Not really," he'd said.

"That's too bad. You're probably missing out on meeting some good people."

He'd given me a contemplative look then. "I don't think I've ever looked at it that way."

"We're not all here just to serve the great Aidan St. Claire," I'd said, giving him a little hip check.

"That's not what I meant."

"I know," I told him, serving him a cheeky grin.

Things don't seem to be going so smoothly at the beauty-supply store, though. I'd better save him.

"You needed some product to help keep your hair styled, remember, babe? Maybe some mousse or some gel?" I yell over to him. I'm not sure why I decided to make it sound like we were together; it certainly wasn't because the woman behind the counter had been batting her eyelashes up at him. But what's done is done.

"Right," he says with a head bob toward me. "My . . . girlfriend over there thought I should try something new."

The marquee board in my brain lights up. He said *girlfriend*! But I mentally turn it off and remind myself it's not true and that Aidan was just following my lead.

But I can't stop the swirling in my lower belly. I know it's not true, and by the reddening of the tips of his ears I can see from where I'm standing, it's obvious Aidan's body is reacting to the lie.

Even still, it makes me wonder what it would be like to date Aidan St. Claire? Which is a dumb question because I already know the answer. It would be hard. I'd never know where I stood. I'd always have to take the lead. He'd never be able to express how he feels, not until I'd used my special gift/ toxic trait on him. And then he'd break my heart and marry the next woman he meets.

I know myself. I always think, *This time it'll be different. This time I'll finally hear someone tell me he loves me. This time I'll get all the things I want from a relationship.* I'm the definition of insanity — doing the same thing over and over again and expecting a different result. Well, not anymore.

Aidan gets a full education in the types of products the beauty supply store has to offer, the woman taking him around to different aisles and chatting him up as she goes. He asks pertinent questions and seems to be holding his own just fine.

By the time we leave, I have a bagful of stuff, including some of the things the purple-haired woman showed to Aidan.

"You did well, young Padawan," I say as we get into my sedan and buckle our seat belts. It's a totally overused and cliché thing to say, but I do it anyway.

"Are we done yet?" he asks.

I give him a smirk. "Not even close."

"Mom's freaking out," my sister Olivia says to me over the phone as I'm sitting on the pink couch in my pj's.

I was just about to watch a Turkish drama in an attempt to shut my brain off after the long day I've had.

Things went pretty well with Aidan for the rest of our stops. At least I felt like they did. One of the stops was Target, where I made him ask more than one employee where to find things I was looking for. I knew exactly where they were, because I heart Target, but it was much more fun to make him ask.

"Wouldn't it be easier if we just found it ourselves?" he'd asked me after he'd awkwardly approached a young teen boy in a red shirt for help.

"You're just mad because I made you ask him where to find the tampons," I'd said. I could have gone easy on the guy, but why do that? His future wife will thank me.

"That's not why," he'd said.

"Really? Because I caught that little flinch when you asked the kid."

He'd huffed out a breath. "I did not."

"It's important to be able to ask for help," I'd told him. "You can't just count on yourself all the time."

"Sure you can."

"You needed *my* help, didn't you?"

"Yes, and I asked you for help."

"Yes, but I had to offer it to you first." Even if it had been a joke.

I'd wrapped an arm around his then as he pushed the red cart. "And aren't you grateful every day that I did?"

He'd harrumphed. "Jury's still out." I'd looked over to see a hint of a smile on his lips.

Later on, as we drove back to Aspen Lake, before I dropped him off at the boat store where he'd left his car, he did admit our outing today helped him. I felt very triumphant. I hope he'll still want to talk to me after the next phase of my plan, because it's a doozy.

Then I headed to work, and during one of my breaks, Chantelle was there and she hadn't forgotten about our last conversation like I'd hoped and kept bombarding me with questions. I'm not sure why she cares. In the end, I think I answered enough of her questions to placate her. But she did give me a warning before walking out of the break room in that hip-swinging way she does. She'd said, "Don't you go falling for that man." To which I'd responded, "Duh."

Now I'm on my couch wishing I hadn't picked up the phone, but Olivia so rarely calls me, I was curious.

"Mom is always freaking out," I say to her. "What's got her panties in a bundle now?"

"Gross," Olivia says. Of course, she'd never use such a crass phrase. "She doesn't think we'll get enough money for the barn."

I let out a breath. Do I tell her about the money Aidan is going to give me? No. Even though I feel like I'm making some headway there, there's still no guarantee. We still have so much work to do. It'll have to be more like a game-saving-play-in-the-fourth-quarter type thing.

"We'll get there" is all I offer.

"I hope so," she says. "Both she and Lottie have been saying they might have to sell off part of the farm to help fund it."

"They can't do that," I say, my voice practically squeaking. That thought never occurred to me. That land has been in our family for generations.

"They might have to; they'll lose too much revenue without it."

I close my eyes and shake my head, even if she can't see me.

"So," she continues, "you have any ideas?"

"I'm working on something."

"And that is?"

"I'm," I start but then stop myself. What am I going to tell her? "It's complicated."

"Not that line again."

"What?"

"You always say that," she says.

"No I don't," I say. Why are people calling me out on this? First Chantelle, and now my sister? I guess I can understand with my sister. She's never interested in what's going on in my life. It's easier just to shut the conversation down. I'm still confused about Chantelle.

I let out a long breath. "I've got something in the works, and it if goes to plan, it could help in a big way. But I don't want to get any hopes up, okay?"

"Okay," she says, sounding somewhat mollified.

"What are you doing to help out?" I ask, kind of irritated that it sounds like she's expecting me to do the heavy lifting here. What about Oliver? Is he doing anything? I know Josie's been trying to figure things out too. Her pirate had already donated a wad of cash to the tune of $2,000. No one knew about that one except for Josie and me. Sadly, it hardly made a dent.

"I'm doing a lot of things," Olivia says, sounding defensive. "But it's not easy when I have to run a home and a family, you know."

Of course she'd say that. Like I have all the time in the world and she has none. Maybe if she'd let go of trying to make everything so perfect, she'd have way more time on her hands.

"I know," I tell her. "We're all doing our best."

"Mommy, I need you to wipe my gluteus maximus!" I hear Jonathan's young, squeaky voice scream in the background.

"Gluteus maximus? Really, Olivia?" She's gone too far with that one.

"I've gotta run," she says and then hangs up the phone.

Chapter Sixteen

Jenna Peterson's Guide to Dating Emotionally Unavailable Men:

Trying new things that are deemed uncomfortable may not be well received.

The next Saturday, Aidan is set to meet me at the farm. He was a little skeptical when I'd sent him the text.

Aidan: I don't know. Did you tell your family what I said? They're not going to tar and feather me or something are they?

Me: We don't tar and feather people at Peterson's Pumpkin Patch. We hog-tie them and put them in Rufus's cage.

Aidan: Is Rufus a bull or something?

He sent a GIF of a bull chasing after a man.

Me: No, he's a bunny

He then sent me back a bunch of question marks.

Me: Trust me, you don't want to be in a cage with Rufus. He's very . . . amorous. Your legs will never be the same.

Aidan sent back a row of those green emojis that look like they're about to barf.

Me: Just be there, okay? 8:30 sharp. At the orange building by the entrance. Try not to let anyone see you when you come in.

Aidan: Why?

Me: Just trust me

Aidan: I'm scared

Me: I promise you'll survive

Me: Hopefully

He should be scared, honestly. I sort of am. I'm hoping to do this next phase of my plan without being seen by the sisters. It should be easy to pull off — it should be a busy day, and when it's busy I rarely see either of them unless I venture outside my little building. In fact, on a crazy day, it's rare that I see anyone from my family here in my little orange box.

It's not that they'll be mad at what I'm having Aidan do — it'll just create a lot of questions and assumptions. Mountains out of molehills, remember?

The only person that might work her way over here is Josie, and she's gone for most of the day at her school's carnival. She'd definitely have questions if she knew, so I'm glad this all worked out so well. It's like all the stars aligned for my little plan.

At exactly eight thirty, I hear a couple of taps on my door.

"Hey," I say, opening the door for Aidan and ushering him in.

"Hi," he says, in that gruff tone. He reluctantly comes inside.

"Did anybody see you?" I ask.

He pulls his eyebrows downward. "No," he says, only it comes out as more of a question.

"Good."

I peek my head out the door and look left and right and then left again for good measure. Not seeing anyone, I go back inside and shut the door, locking the dead bolt.

I turn around and lean against the door. It feels very much like I just sneaked a man into my bedroom. I mean, I sort of have.

Aidan gives me questioning eyes. "What's the plan?"

"Yes, the plan," I say, moving away from the door and walking over to the long counter that runs along the structure's side, just under the small ticketing window. I grab a folded orange shirt that I placed there earlier and toss it to him. He catches it with ease, like we practiced this.

"Put that on," I say.

He looks down at the shirt and then back at me, wearing the same shirt. "Why?"

I waggle my eyebrows. "Because today you get to work at Peterson's Pumpkin Patch."

"Doing what?" he says, the shirt flopping around in his hand.

"Selling tickets, of course," I say, pointing to the little window above the counter.

He eyes me, dubiously. "How is this supposed to help?"

"More stranger interaction," I say, and give him a little nod. I'm kind of proud of this one. I think everyone should have to, at some point in their life, work in a customer service-related job. Whether it's waiting tables at a restaurant, working a cash register at a department store, bagging groceries, or selling tickets at a pumpkin patch. It's important to see the other side of things, to understand what people in this position have to deal with. It would make for a much kinder world, in my opinion.

Since it's safe to say Aidan has never had to work at such a job, this is a great way for him to work on his communication issue, because he's going to have to talk to people, over and over and over again.

He lets out a long breath through his nose. "Is there going to be some training here, or are you just going to throw me to the wolves?"

"Of course I'm going to train you; I'm not Satan."

"That's debatable," he says. He takes off his jacket and sets it on one of the office-type chairs we have in this room. And then with one swift move, he reaches a hand over his head, and grabbing a handful of the back of his tan sweater, he pulls it over his head and off his body.

Well, hello there. The marquee board in my head flashes the words at me. I'm like a deer caught in headlights, and I know I should turn and look the other way, but the sight before me is definitely one to behold. A shirtless Aidan, in dark-colored jeans, his beautifully sculpted upper body on full display. I've never been a sucker for abs, but hot damn I think I just became a fan.

I go to swallow, because I think I've forgotten how to, and that's when I realize I'm staring. And my mouth is open. And Aidan St. Claire has a little smirk on his face because he caught me.

I slam my jaw shut and quickly look away, turning my back to him. I hear him rustling around as he puts the shirt on, and when I feel like it's safe, I turn back around.

In the few seconds with my back turned, I had the following pep talk with myself.

Me: *Get ahold of yourself, Jenna!*

My ovaries: *But did you see his stomach?*

Me: *He insulted my family's farm! Never forget that!*

My ovaries: *Oh, let that go. Remember those forearms and that butt?*

Me: *Shut up!*

As pep talks go, it was mostly a failure. Even touching the gold band on my necklace isn't offering any strength. *Save me, Grandma P!*

I sniffle, and then give Aidan a big, cheesy grin. "You ready?"

"I guess," he says, his tone flat. There are remnants of a smirk on those lips of his.

We spend the next half hour before opening going over how to use the computer, how to take the money, things he can upsell people on—like professional pictures in the patch—and remembering to mention the donation jar.

"You have to be your nicest self, okay?" I say to him. "I can't have word getting back to my mom and aunt that some meanie at the ticket booth ruined someone's experience. I really can't have them finding out about this at all." I point to myself and then to him.

"Why?" he asks, his brow wrinkling.

"Because they will ask me a million questions, that's why."

"Okay," he says, drawing out the word.

He wouldn't understand if I tried to explain it to him. My family is . . . impossible.

At nine o'clock, I unlock the ticketing window and open it to a line already ten people deep. I help the first couple of people so Aidan can get the hang of how we do things around here, and then I turn it over to him.

"Wait," I say before switching places with him. "I forgot one thing."

I open a drawer under the counter and pull out my pièce de résistance: an orange beret.

"There's no way," he starts.

"You have to," I say. "It's the uniform." I reach up and place it on his head. And then I have to suck my lips between my teeth because I might lose it.

"Is this payback for laughing at your accent?" he deadpans, the hat looking ridiculous on him.

I snort out a laugh. "That wasn't my plan, but it's not a bad side effect."

He closes his eyes and takes a breath.

"Your audience awaits you," I say as I wave my hand at the window.

He reluctantly steps up to it. "Welcome to Peterson's Pumpkin Patch," he says, his tone still gruff. And he's not doing it with a smile on his face like I showed him, but he's doing it, and that's enough.

"You're free to go," I say to him after making him work for three hours. Right around noon there tends to be a lull in customers, so it's a good time to let him go.

"How did I do?" he asks, holding out his palms toward me.

I bob my head to the side. "I mean, you could have been a little more pumpkiny, but you did all right." I give him a cheeky smile.

"I'll have to work on that," he says, the corner of his mouth lifting up.

"I'm not sure being pumpkiny is what you need for the conference."

"Probably not," he says.

"But you did talk to a lot of people today. How do you feel?"

"Tired," he says. "It was harder than I thought it would be."

"It is, isn't it?"

I reach up and take the orange beret off his head. Without thinking, I reach up again and run my fingers through his thick, dark hair in an attempt to try and fix the pieces that are standing up. He lets out a little moan, as if he likes it.

"Sorry," I say, shaking my head as I quickly pull my hand away, not sure what got into me just now. *Yes, you are – you've wanted to touch his hair since you met him.* I hate my brain.

"I'll just take this off," he says after clearing his throat. He reaches for the bottom of the T-shirt.

"No," I say to stop him. I don't need to see *all that* again. "You can keep it. A little something to remember the farm you hate so much."

He cocks his head to the side, an annoyed look on his face. "I never said I hated it."

"I'm pretty sure you did."

"I didn't," he says. "I still don't know why I even brought it up with you."

"Because you meant it."

"No." He shakes his head. "I mean, at the time. But I don't know what compelled me to tell you. I guess I wanted to talk to you more."

I scrunch my face at him, giving him a bemused smile. "By insulting my family farm?"

"I didn't know it was your family's farm at the time."

163

I shake my head at him, chuckling. "Well, I mean, it worked. I did stay and talk with you longer, didn't I?" That evening at the Eagle's Den seems like so long ago.

"Clearly I needed help."

"Yes, well, that's what I'm here for." That and $5,000. Funny—I tend to forget about that when I'm with him.

"I think it's working," he says.

"Well, you haven't gotten to the third part of my plan," I say.

"Is it worse than this?" He points to the ticketing window, a soft breeze blowing through it.

"Oh yeah." I bob my head up and down. "It's much worse."

"Excellent."

Later that afternoon, after the pumpkin patch has closed, I stand next to Josie, watching her pirate boyfriend take his daughter on a tractor ride. It's picturesque with the sun setting behind him, and Josie is watching them with so much love on her face. She kind of looks like the heart-eyes emoji.

Reece looks over our way and smiles big; you can see he's got it bad for my cousin, which makes me happy and sad at the same time. Happy because I think Josie has finally found the right man for her, and sad because things will change. We'll always be close, I know that, but it won't be like it used to be.

It's weird, when she was engaged to her ex, Trevor, I could never picture it. I could never see the two of them together. But I can see her and Reece together, almost as clear as day.

"I'm happy for you, Jo Jo," I tell her.

"I'm happy for me too," she says, giving me a smile.

I let out a giggle. "Looks like someone's going to get her freak on."

She gives me duck lips, her brows pulling inward. "By that, I'm sure you mean dancing."

"That's exactly what I mean." I wiggle my eyebrows at her. "Wink, wink, nudge, nudge, Bob's your uncle," I say in a British accent, which I'd always thought I was good at doing but am now doubting because of Aidan. It makes me smile, remembering him laughing like he did.

"Oh my gosh," Josie says in a half whisper. "Stop it. You know the sisters are nearby."

We both look around to see if mentioning them had conjured them up, but it looks like that particular trick doesn't work every time, because they are nowhere to be seen.

"I can't wait to hear what the sisters have to say about you 'dancing' with the pirate," I say to her.

She rolls her eyes at me. "Maybe you should *dance* with someone."

"Maybe I already am," I say. I'm not sure why I say it—I'm not dancing literally, or even metaphorically, with anyone.

She lifts one eyebrow, surprised. "Do tell," she says.

Do I tell her about Aidan? Maybe not. I'm not dancing with him, but I am spending time with him. And sure, there's the money for the barn and all that, but that's not why he keeps popping into my mind, his name in bright lights on that marquee board in my head. I don't know if it was the abs display earlier that sealed the deal—which would make me very superficial—or the way it felt to run my fingers through his hair, but despite all the ways I tried to protect myself, to warn myself . . . I like him. Not even what he said about the farm bothers me anymore.

I've done it again. I've caught feelings for an emotionally unavailable man. I don't want to tell Josie. I don't even want to say the words aloud.

I give her a little smile. "I will when the time is right." Which will probably be never. I just have to make it through the next few weeks, and then I'll probably never see Aidan St. Claire again.

She tilts her head, drawing her brows inward. "What's going on with you?"

I take a breath. "I'm good. I promise."

It's a lie. I'm not good. Not at all.

Chapter Seventeen

Jenna Peterson's Guide to Dating Emotionally Unavailable Men:

Be prepared for broken plans. They will happen often.

I had to reschedule the third part of my plan for Aidan until the following Sunday because the morning after I made him work on the farm, I got a text from him saying he had to go out of town and that he'd probably be back in a week.

I was annoyed with myself because my stomach sank when I saw the words on my screen. And I actually wondered what I was going to do without him for a whole week. Which was so ridiculous. I haven't even known him that long, and yet I've gotten used to having him around.

I told myself this was good. I could take the week and work on un-catching feelings for him. I even concocted a plan. It wasn't all that detailed—I was just going to think about something else anytime he popped into my mind. A little brain reframing. I was going to be feelings-free by the time he got back.

But then he made it easy on me. I'd texted him right after I got his message, asking him if everything was okay, and I never heard from him. Not once, the entire week. He couldn't be bothered to even text back with a thumbs-up.

It shouldn't have upset me. It's not like Aidan and I were anything but a business transaction. Only it seemed, at least to me, like we were becoming friends. We'd been hanging out, texting pretty frequently, and then . . . nothing.

It was a good reminder. A reminder that Aidan St. Claire is not the kind of man I want in my life. I want someone open and willing to tell me things. Not someone I have to pry information out of.

I went about the week with my head held high and a smile on my face. Well, that's what I'd planned to do. Instead, Chantelle told me I was acting like a troll, and Heather—sweet, never-has-a-mean-thing-to-say Heather—gave me mother face, which is something akin to teacher face, only worse because it was more pitying, and basically agreed with Chantelle.

I'm usually good at faking it until I make it, but apparently not this time. I don't know why this thing with Aidan hurt so much. Maybe it was more that I was mad at myself for getting caught up in the first place. Fool me once—or I guess in my case *five times*—and all that. Matthew, Brian, Garrett, Cam, and now Aidan. Will I ever learn? At least I can't put Aidan in the foolishly dated department.

I think sometimes the universe puts you in the same situations again to see if you're still an idiot. Clearly, I am.

On Saturday, when I still hadn't heard a word from him, I did start to wonder if something had happened. Like, maybe I'd spent this whole week annoyed with him and he'd been lying in a coma. Or maybe he'd driven off a cliff and survived but no one knew and he had to hike his way out of the mountains, fighting off wolves and bears and eating leaves to survive.

But then, that night, I got a text from him, and all it said was:

Aidan: Heading back tonight. Are we on for Monday?

So, no coma or fighting off wild animals. Not even an apology for ghosting me this week; no asking me how I've been. Just a quick text reminding me that I have a job to do.

Even though I wanted to text back something snide or passive-aggressive — I thought up some really good ones — all I sent back was one word: *Sure.*

But then I had to send him instructions on where to meet me and what time, so my one-word you-mean-nothing-to-me text didn't have quite the effect I was aiming for.

It's fine. It really is. It's better this way. He's not the kind of man I need in my life, and this was all a really good reminder.

Now it's Sunday evening and instead of going home and snuggling up with Can Yaman, I find myself walking around the farm. It's chilly, but the slightly sweet scent of hay in the breeze fills me with comfort. The farm life may not be for me anymore, but I still love it.

I spy my dad and uncle working on a smaller utility tractor as I pass the barn where we house them. They look like an advertisement for farming in their flannels and overalls. It's not a look they put on just for the pumpkin patch either. It's everyday wear for them.

"Hey, Little Pumpkin," my dad says when he sees me standing at the entrance. He moves away from the engine they were both leaning over, a portable work lamp giving them enough light to see in the old barn.

Grandfather Peterson helped build this barn many years ago. Later, a loft was installed so we could store things, and my uncle put a punching bag up there for Josie that I've yet to take advantage of. She tells me it's good for the soul. I could use a little soul searching by way of punching.

"Hey, Dad; hey, Uncle Charles. How's it going in here?" I gesture toward the tractor.

"Oh, you know, just working on this old girl," my uncle Charles says, patting one of the massive back tires with the yellow rim.

"What're you up to?" my dad asks me.

"I was just walking around, doing some thinking." I give him a smile.

"It's the best place for it," he says, giving me a wink.

That's something he and I have in common — needing fresh air for our souls. My mom and Olivia are so busy thinking, so busy planning their next move that they don't have time to mosey around here contemplating. Most often, and especially during the season, you can find Dana Peterson moving around this place like a crack-fed Energizer Bunny.

"What's on your mind?" my dad asks me.

"Just life," I say.

"Well, come on in and stay for a bit," my dad says.

I walk toward them, feeling the gravel shift under my feet.

"What's wrong with the tractor?"

"I thought it was a spark plug, but it looks like it might be a bigger issue," Uncle Charles says.

"Maybe something with the fuel system," my dad says to me.

I'm no use here. I used to try to help them fix engines when I was younger, but I think I got in the way more than anything.

Uncle Charles stands up. "I think I need to go grab a flashlight so we can get a better look." He wipes his hands on his overalls, which are already fairly stained.

"Good idea," my dad tells him.

"How's life?" he asks me as Uncle Charles leaves.

I shrug one shoulder, even though he's bent over now, fiddling with the engine, so he can't see me. "It's good," I tell him.

"So then, what's up?"

I think about that for a second, my mind a bunch of spinning thoughts. "Do you ever do the same thing over and over again, hoping for a different result?"

"Oh, sure," he says. "Every single day that I wake up married to your mom." He looks over at me as he gives me a big belly laugh.

I laugh too. "I'm going to tell her you said that."

"Don't you dare. You know I love your mom more than anything."

I do know that. Thank goodness they found each other. They're like the perfect match: my mom with her let's-run-the-world attitude, and my dad more the type that believes things will work out how they're supposed to. Even with the way they handle the barn. My mom made plans, and my dad . . . well, he's more hopeful, I suppose.

"So, what have you been doing over and over again, hoping for different results?"

I debate telling him but then decide what the heck. "Oh, you know. Just the kind of people I let into my life."

"You mean men?"

"Yes, Dad," I say, my tone sarcastic. "That's what I mean."

"What's the problem there?"

I sigh. "I guess I just seem to always attract the same type of guy."

"Well, the last bunch you've brought around were a bunch of idiots," he says.

"That's the type," I say on a laugh. Maybe I should take it as a sign when not one person in my family has liked anyone I've brought home. But it's not like Josie has had a bunch of luck there either, and she found a good one. At least the sisters are finally starting to warm up to Reece.

"You attract idiots?"

"I guess so," I say.

He stands up to his full height and turns toward me. "You want some advice?"

"Sure."

"Stop trying to fix things."

"What?" I ask him, confused.

"You're not going to want to hear this, but you're more like your mom than you realize."

"Take that back," I say. I'm teasing him, but my insides did squirm a little when he said that, and I could feel my defenses rising.

"I wish I could," he says, teasing back. "But it's the truth. You're stubborn like her. And determined."

"I am not."

"When you want something, you are. When you lived here, you were always following me around, asking me questions and trying to help me fix things."

"I'm inquisitive."

"Yes, and it could be extremely annoying when you were younger."

"Dad," I chide.

He holds his dirty, oil-stained hands up, palms toward me. "It's not a bad thing. But maybe sometimes things don't need to be fixed, or they aren't fixable."

"I'm assuming you're talking about people."

He nods his head, just once.

I stare at him, his words bouncing around in my head. Is it possible that rather than people opening up to me on their own, my toxic trait is that I force it out of them by asking questions? Am I like a serial questioner?

"You're good at asking the right questions; it's a talent," he says like he's just read my thoughts. "But it's also not your job."

It's not my job . . .

"When did you get to be so smart?" I ask him after a few beats of silence.

"Don't tell your mom. If she knew, she'd be asking me to do everything around here." He gives me a smile then, and I smile back.

Chapter Eighteen

Jenna Peterson's Guide to Dating Emotionally Unavailable Men:

Relationships are hard, but when you're with someone who's emotionally unavailable, they can be draining. Like the suck-the-life-out-of-you kind of draining.

I may not have been able to fake it until I made it while Aidan was gone, but I'm doing a bang-up job right now with him. In fact, I'm acting like the last week didn't happen. My feelings are still hurt, of course. But that's on me. Aidan's done nothing wrong. He's never promised me anything. And it's for the best, really. I will do the job he asked me to do, with no other expectations of him except that I get paid when I'm done.

For Aidan's part, the last week seems to have taken a toll on him. I briefly wondered if my coma story might have been real. Although I doubt he'd be standing here with me, outside the Carson City community center, if it had been. Seems like something you don't just snap back from in a week's time.

But something definitely went down. He's got dark circles under his eyes, and his face seems a little pale. And he looks . . . weary.

My brain starts firing off questions when I first see him, wanting to get to the bottom of things. But I've been thinking a lot about what my dad said last night. The truth is, when people want to talk to you, they will. So I'm going to try harder to let that happen naturally instead of taking over asking questions like I always do.

Aidan lets out a sigh as he opens the door and we walk into the building. It smells like new paint and carpet. Just inside the doors, in the large entry space, long rectangular tables are set up into a square with chairs on both the inside and outside, and people are gathered around, some chatting in groups, some on their own looking at their phones. One man, an older gentleman, looks to be staring at a wall.

"What is this?" Aidan asks in his gruff tone. It's got a side of extra grumpy today. He's wearing the leather jacket he wore when we first met. And the same scowl too.

"Speed dating," I say, smiling at him and holding out a hand toward the action in front of us.

It's actually harder to find in-person speed dating these days with all the online dating sites. They even do online speed dating. But the actual face-to-face version still exists, even in Carson City. By the looks of things—if the number of gray heads is any indication—this might be more for people who don't get online all that often or maybe not at all. It doesn't matter, though. We're not here to meet people. We're here to practice talking to them. Well, Aidan is at least. It's a genius plan.

Aidan looks at me, then looks at the speed dating setup, and then back at me. Without a word, he pivots on the balls of his feet and walks back out the door we just came in.

"Aidan?" I call after him as I follow him out the door. "What are you doing?"

He rubs a hand down his face. "I'm not doing this."

"What? Why?" I ask him. I'd expected some pushback, since that's how he's been every time I've made him try something new, but an outright rejection is unexpected.

"I don't think this will help."

"What do you mean? It's perfect," I say, pointing toward the door we just exited. "You get to talk to people, rapid-fire style. And with real questions, not 'How many tickets today?' like at the farm."

He closes his eyes and takes in a breath. I think he might come around, but he says, "Can we do something else tonight instead?"

"Well, I mean, we're running out of time here. Your conference is in a few weeks."

"I know, but last week was . . . I . . ." He stops talking, running a hand down the back of his head this time and letting it hang there on his neck. "I guess I'm not in the frame of mind to chat with strangers."

My brain starts firing off questions. *Why? What happened? What's going on?* I tell it to be quiet and remind it that we are trying something different this time.

"But we—"

He drops his hand to his side and flexes it before relaxing. "I think I need to decompress."

"Okay," I say. I can tell I won't be changing his mind. He looks so sad, so worn out. *Ask him! Ask him!* my brain is practically screaming at me. But I'm not going to ask him. I'm going to mind my own business.

"I'll think of something else," I tell him, giving him my best understanding smile. "I'll text you when I think of something." I pull the keys out of my purse to get ready to head to my car.

"Go on a drive with me," he says, out of the blue.

"What?"

"I . . . I just . . . please," he says, his lips pulled downward, his blue eyes looking almost gray in the fading sun.

I probably shouldn't. I don't know how the me that's trying not to ask so many questions is going to be able to sit in a car with this man for who knows how long and keep my mouth shut. Silence is icky, not golden. But there's something about him, the way he looks right now, so drained, so bone-tired. I know I won't say no.

I put my keys back in my purse. "Okay, sure," I tell him.

I follow him to his car, a four-door shiny black Mercedes. I've never been in his car before. We've mostly just met at places, or I've driven, like when I made him run errands with me.

He opens the door for me, which feels weird but also kind of nice. It's been a long time since someone did that for me. I suppose it's probably one of those outdated traditions for most people. Not in the house I grew up in, though. My dad has always opened any door for my mom.

I slide into the dark-gray leather seat as Aidan shuts my door and then buckle myself in while he walks around the car and gets in the other side.

"Where are we going?" I ask once he's started up the engine with a press of a button.

"I don't know," he says.

"Okay," I say. I'm okay with that. I remember going on drives when I was dating Matthew. He never had a set destination. He just wanted to be on the road.

We take off down Stewart Street, and when he turns right onto Highway 50, I know where we're going, or at least I know where we're heading. Aspen Lake. Which is where I live. But now my car is parked at the community center in Carson City. I guess, somehow, we'll figure that all out later.

We ride in silence with only the hum of the engine as our soundtrack. The silence isn't easy, but I tell myself to relax into the luxury that is Aidan's car, keeping my eyes on the road as we drive.

I look over at Aidan for a moment, watching the way he focuses on the road, one hand on the steering wheel and the other lying on the armrest between us.

"I'm sorry," he finally says. I'm assuming for not wanting to do tonight's activity.

"It's fine," I say, and I push all the sincerity I can into those two words. It really is fine. It wasn't like I was disappointed to leave the speed dating. Although maybe I would have met the silver fox of my dreams if we'd stayed. Guess I'll never know.

"Last week," he says, and then goes silent, keeping his eyes on the road in front of us.

I open my mouth to say *Last week what?* but then stop myself.

He swallows. "Last week, I flew to San Francisco."

"Okay," I say, just to let him know I'm listening.

"My brother, Jake. He's been sort of missing for a while." He pauses and I worry that maybe he's not going to keep talking, which would be very frustrating. *Keep your questions to yourself, Jenna.*

"Not like a *missing person* kind of thing where I thought the police should get involved, but a few months ago when it had been over a year since either me or my mom or dad had heard from him, I hired someone to investigate the situation."

"Wow," I say. "I'm assuming they found him."

I look over to see him dip his chin, just once, his eyes focused on the road. "They did."

"Was . . . was he okay?" I can't help the question—it just popped out of my mouth. I'm not going to be hard on myself; this is the first time in pretty much my entire life I've attempted this. Rome wasn't built in a day, and I should give myself at least that long to work through my need to know everything. I heard it took over a million days to build Rome, and it could take me just as long. Or possibly longer.

"No," he says, simply.

"I'm sorry," I say, wondering how *not* okay his brother is. Like unalive-not-okay? It does make sense now, why he didn't text me back and was radio silent the entire week. He was going through a lot.

"He was found living on the streets," he continues. "So high, he didn't know where he was and barely knew *who* he was."

"Oh, Aidan," I say, feeling my throat grow thick. I swallow it down. How awful that must have been, to deal with that. And I was over here thinking about my hurt little feelings because he didn't text me back. In my defense, I had no idea. But now it feels trivial in comparison.

His arm is still lying between us, so I do something that might be stupid, but it feels like a natural thing to do. I reach over and place my hand on top of his, wrapping my fingers around his palm. I give him a little squeeze. I'm about to let go since this is just supposed to be a quick act of comfort, but before I can, he flips his hand around and wraps his fingers around mine, his thumb starts making an up-and-down pattern over my skin.

I look down at our connected hands and then up at his face, my heart quickening to an erratic pace at his touch. It's only a friendly thing; I know that. He needs comfort, and I'm here to give it to him. But . . . I don't hate it. His hand is warm, and it practically engulfs mine. It's not rough, like how my dad's farmer hands feel. But it's not soft either.

"What happened after he was found?" I ask, after having to make a concerted effort to swallow. *Don't read into this, Jenna. Do. Not.*

"They took him to a local shelter, and that's where I picked him up Sunday morning."

He keeps that pattern on my hand going, his thumb moving up and down over the top of mine. If we were dating, I'd pull his hand into my lap and wrap my other arm around his bicep. I feel like I want to do that now, like I want him to be closer to me, but I don't. Because that would be stupid.

"What happened after you picked him up?" I've gone full Jenna here, and I'm okay with it. I'll start building Rome tomorrow.

"I got him cleaned up and then spent the rest of the week finding a rehab facility for him."

"Did you find one?"

"I did," he says. "He wasn't happy about it. But that was hopefully the withdrawal talking."

"I'm sure," I say. I can only assume, as I have no experience in this arena. I grew up on a farm. The only rehabilitation that was happening there was when wild animals would get caught in the fence around the property and we'd try to help the ones we could before releasing them back into the wild.

He lets go of my hand and puts both of his on the steering wheel to turn off onto a road I've never been on. The road starts to curve and bend as we slowly work our way up one of the many mountains that make up Aspen Lake. I put my hand back in my lap and try not to think about how bare it feels now.

"Do you think he'll be okay?" I look over at him.

He lifts a shoulder and drops it. "I don't know. I hope so."

"He's lucky to have you," I say.

He sighs, but it sounds more like a deep grumble in his chest. "I should have done more."

"No," I say, shaking my head, even though I know he can't see me as he keeps his focus on the winding road in front of us. "I don't know the whole story, but I'm pretty sure it wasn't your choices that got your brother in the situation he's in. That was a series of choices on his part."

"I could have helped, though. This has been going on for a while. He started getting into stuff not long after our dad left."

"Aidan," I say, reaching up to touch his arm. "It's not your job to take care of everyone."

He glances over at me this time, just briefly, and then back to the road. "I know," he says.

"And even if you did everything in your power to help him, the outcome might have been exactly the same."

He nods his head, but I don't think he believes me. But just like it's not Aidan's job to fix his brother, it's not my job to make him see that. It's hard, though, to not want to. I guess we're the same that way. I'm not trying to take care of everyone, but I am always trying to fix things. It's exhausting, really.

It's silent for a bit, except for the engine. The bright lights of his car reflect off the road and the branches of tall evergreen trees lining the streets.

"Do you mind if we stop somewhere?" he asks me.

"I don't mind," I say, wondering where that could possibly be.

About a minute later, he turns down a long driveway that winds up to a beautiful older-looking house. Aidan parks the car in the empty driveway, turns off the ignition, and unhooks his seat belt.

"Where are we?" I ask, looking at him.

"This is where I grew up," he says. "My grandparents' house. My mom lives here now."

Chapter Nineteen

Jenna Peterson's Guide to Dating Emotionally Unavailable Men:

You will rarely get an invite to meet his parents. So take it as a win if you do.

This is his mom's house?

"Um, okay. Did you need to grab something?" I ask him. "I can wait in the car."

"No, come in," he says. "I want you to meet her."

I nod my head before undoing my seat belt and opening my car door. I take a big breath of the cold mountain air as we walk toward a large oak front door with a wreath of fall leaves hanging on it. The giant inhale wasn't just because I have to breathe to live—I also needed something to steady me.

This is not where I pictured myself tonight. Aidan and I are supposed to be at a speed dating thing right now. I'm supposed to be helping him be more comfortable around people, but instead we're at his childhood home and I'm about to meet his mother.

I shouldn't feel nervous about this because we're not dating. This isn't some meet-the-parents situation where there's a lot riding on whether his family likes me and I like them. But, despite knowing that, I do feel a little anxious right now.

But here's the honest truth: I've never met the parents of someone I've dated. I know, it sounds strange even to me. Like, with every guy I've ever dated, not one has taken me home to meet his parents. That seems ridiculous, right? Yet . . . it's true. Not Matthew, Brian, Garrett, or Cam, or any other guy before them, ever brought me home to meet dear Mom and Dad. Well, I guess the one exception is Brian. I did meet his parents, but that was only because we'd been out to dinner one night and had run into them. It was awkward, to say the least. And when they asked him to introduce me (yes, they had to ask), he told them I was his *friend*. We'd been dating for nearly six months when this happened. I'd love to say that was the beginning of the end, but it wasn't.

I swallow as Aidan takes his keys out of his jacket pocket and uses one of them to open the door. He knocks on the open door as we walk inside.

"Mom?" he calls out.

"I'm in here," a voice says, and we walk down a hallway until it opens up to a lovely farmhouse kitchen on the right and a brightly decorated living room on the left. A woman with thick, dark hair stands up from a brown leather recliner. Her hair is the same color as Aidan's, although it probably isn't all natural anymore, and she has oval-shaped glasses on her face.

"It's my boy," she says as we walk into the room. She's a beautiful woman, with the same color eyes as Aidan's, the same face shape, only slightly rounder, and a much bigger and easier smile on her face than I've ever seen on her son, except for the times I've made him laugh. "And you brought a guest." She walks toward us, giving Aidan a quick side hug and then reaching a hand out toward me.

"This is Jenna," he says to his mom, by way of introduction. "And this is my mom, Jackie."

I reach out and take her hand. It feels warm, and she gives mine a little squeeze as we shake. "Jenna," she says. "I've heard so much about you."

I'm taken aback by this declaration as she lets go of my hand. I look to Aidan, who's looking at something across the room. "You have?" I say to her.

"Oh, yes," she says. "Aidan's told me how you're helping him."

"He did?"

Aidan's eyes finally meet mine, and he gives me one of his signature grins, where his lips pull up only slightly.

"Yes," she says. "Heaven knows he needs all the help he can get."

"Mom," he says, his tone sounding slightly chastising.

"Well, you do," she says, and then pushes her lips out at him, very duck-like. I smile because I've only known Jackie for maybe three minutes and I already like her. What was I worried about?

"Do you want something to drink?" she asks as she walks into the kitchen.

"I'd love some water," I tell her.

She walks over to one of the tall white cabinets in her beautiful kitchen and grabs two clear glasses and then carries them over to a fridge with custom panel doors matching her cabinetry. She fills each cup with ice and water from the dispenser on the door.

It's very different from the kitchen in Aidan's house, and I'm not sure which design I like better. But I love the homeyness of this one. How welcoming it feels.

"I love your kitchen," I say as she hands me the full glass.

"Thank you," she says, handing the other one to Aidan. "I remodeled it last year. It needed an update."

"I love all the color in your living room too."

"Thank you," she says. "I love color. I've been trying to get Aidan to add color to his house since he built the place." She looks at him and gives him a teasing smile. "Do you know, a couple of weeks ago, out of the blue, he called me and asked me to come over and brighten his place up? I was so excited. All that gray he had going on was so boring."

I roll my lips between my teeth as I look at Aidan. "Did he," I say more as a statement than a question.

"He did," she confirms. "I don't know what made him do it, but it's much better now."

"Indeed," I say, giving Aidan a very crap-eating grin.

"Well," Aidan says, reaching up and rubbing his brow. "This was a mistake."

Jackie gives her son a curious look before shrugging it off, and I shake my head at him as she ushers us into the living room and we all take a seat. Jackie back in her brown leather chair, and Aidan and I on a matching sofa, kitty-corner to her.

"So, what brings you here?" she asks.

"I just wanted to drop by," Aidan says. He's still wearing his jacket, which leads me to believe this will be a short visit. "I hadn't seen you since I got back from San Francisco."

Jackie's face drops just a little. "Well, I'm glad you're back and safe. I wish you would have let me go with you, though."

"You didn't need to see all that," he says. "It's better this way."

She nods her head before she holds up a finger like she just remembered something. "Before I forget, can you do me a favor while you're here?"

"Of course," he says.

"I need you to pull a box out of the attic for me."

He eyes her, but then like the obedient son he seems to be, he stands up from the couch. "What do you need?"

"It's over in the southwest corner, and it's got a label on it that says *Sewing*," she says. "There's a dress in there that I've wanted to fix for years, and I think I'm going to do it."

"Sure. No problem," he says. He looks to me. "Do you mind?"

"No," I say, shaking my head at him.

"Yes, go on," Jackie says, shooing him out with her hand. "Jenna will be just fine with me."

"So, tell me about yourself," Jackie says, once Aidan is gone.

"Um . . . what do you want to know?"

"Did you grow up around here?"

"I grew up on a farm in Carson City. Peterson's Pumpkin Patch. Have you heard of it?" I ask when her eyes light up with recognition at my mentioning the farm.

"Of course," she says. "I've been there a few times. Best apple cider on the planet."

I smile at her. Our cider is amazing.

"Do you work on the farm?"

"No, I'm an aesthetician at the Aspen Lake Lodge," I say. "I do work weekends at the farm during the busy season."

"So right now?"

"Yes," I say, nodding my head.

"Aidan told me you found the money his grandpa and grandma gave him."

"I did," I say, reaching up and touching the gold ring around my neck. "I had a feeling it was special and so I took a chance."

"I'm glad you did," she says. She looks down at her hands sitting in her lap, her fingers weaved together. "Can I ask you something?"

"Sure," I say, a trickle of unease moving down my back at what that question might be.

Her eyes meet mine again. "Did Aidan tell you about his brother, Jacob?"

"Um . . . ," I say, looking around the room, wondering how I should answer this. "Yeah, he told me a little about him."

She bobs her head while looking at me, her lips slowly pulling into a grin. "I never thought I'd see the day."

"I'm sorry?" I say, not understanding.

"You've gotten through that rough exterior of his."

"I have?"

"The only person Aidan talks about Jake with is me," she says. "Until now, I guess." She gives me a smile. "And I don't think I'm even getting the full story, like he's trying to protect me."

I nod, because I'm sure that's exactly what he's doing.

"You're good for him," she says, pointing a finger at me.

"Oh . . . well," I stutter out the words. "We're not together or anything, Ms. St. Claire." I don't want to lead her to believe there's something there that's not. And even though Aidan opened up in a big way tonight, even without my normal prodding, it doesn't mean something with him would be right for me.

It's not like it's an option anyway; there's no evidence he has any feelings for me. All physical contact has been initiated by me, and up until tonight, most nonphysical connection has been started by me as well. That doesn't give me a lot of confidence in that area.

She shakes her head. "You can call me Jackie."

"Okay," I say.

"You may not be together, but you're still good for him."

"I don't know about that."

She takes in a breath. "Trust me, you are. And all the stuff you've been doing, I think it's working."

Oh, yes. The job I'm doing for him. That makes more sense. I feel stupid now that I mentioned dating. *Really smooth, Jenna.*

"Well, I hope so," I say. I briefly wonder if he told her about the money he's offered to pay me. Somehow, I don't think so.

Steps can be heard on the stairs, and not long after that, in walks Aidan carrying a medium-size box in his hands.

"Where should I put it?" he asks.

"Oh, just on the table is fine," she says.

He sets it down and then turns to me. "Ready to go? I need to get you back to your car."

"Um . . . sure," I say, standing up from the couch.

"Well, that was a quick visit." Jackie gets up from her chair. "I'm glad you stopped by." She gives Aidan another hug and then follows us down the hall toward that big oak door.

"It was great to meet you," I say to Jackie as Aidan and I exit.

"You too," she says.

Chapter Twenty

Jenna Peterson's Guide to Dating Emotionally Unavailable Men:

Emotionally unavailable men are resistant to change. Ease
them in slowly.

Aidan: What are you doing tomorrow afternoon?

"Put your phone down. We need to talk," Chantelle says as
she walks into the break room.

I jump in my seat at the sound of her voice and then
quickly place my phone facedown in my lap.

She gives me an accusatory side-eye. "What are you
hiding?" She's got on her purple scrubs today, and they really
make her dark eyes pop. Even when they're glaring at me. It's
the first time I've seen her today — the spa has been busy with
lodge guests.

"Nothing," I say. "You just scared me."

She doesn't believe me. I can tell by the duck lips and
squinting eyes she's now giving me. She's not wrong. I was
hiding my conversation with Aidan. I don't need her judgment,
or any more warnings from her. And now I want her to leave so
I can answer his question because I'm curious.

Did he come up with an idea for something we could do? Something to help him since the speed dating thing didn't happen? That was such a perfect idea. Unfortunately, there won't be another one for a while, and then it will be too late. Maybe I could find us a gala to crash, or even some sort of party.

We talked about it on the way to get my car after leaving his mom's house. Well, really it was mostly me wanting to discuss it. Aidan, maybe after seeing his mom, seemed more like himself. At least he seemed less weary.

"We missed our chance," I'd told him once we'd driven down the mountain his mom lived on, and I once again had phone service to access the internet and look up the next event.

"With what?" he'd asked me.

"With speed dating. They won't have another one for three weeks."

"Too bad," he'd said, and not in a tone that made me think he actually meant it.

I'd ignored him. "Now I have no idea what we can do."

"I'm sure you'll figure something out," he'd said.

"I'm assuming more role-playing is a no go." This had come out as more of a plea than a statement.

"That depends."

"On what?"

"On what accent you want to try on me this time. There are some pretty amazing yacht manufacturers in France. Care to attempt that one?"

"So you can laugh at me again?" I'd given him my best glare then, but his eyes were on the road. And when he chuckled at my comment, surprisingly, I didn't feel that little stomach dip. Nope, this time it was more like a flip-flop. And some butterflies joined the party too.

I don't know if it was how he opened up to me about his brother, or the fact that he wanted me to meet his mom, but the feelings I'd been burying over the past week came rushing back, and it's looking even bigger this time. I have a full-blown crush on the man.

I couldn't fall asleep that night, after he dropped me off and we both drove back to Aspen Lake. I'd tossed and turned, trying to figure out how to talk myself down. Then I'd realized I couldn't do this on my own anymore. So I sent Josie a text.

Me: Talk me down.

It was only thirty seconds before my phone vibrated in my hand.

"What's going on?" she'd asked, as soon as I'd said hello.

"I'm an idiot, that's what."

"What happened?"

So I told her. I told her the whole thing. Everything from when I first met Aidan and he'd insulted our family farm (she gasped at that) to the $5,000 (she'd gasped at that too) and then up to earlier that night and what happened. I brought her fully up to speed. Except I'd left out details about his brother because it didn't feel like it was my story to tell.

It felt good to finally tell someone; I'd been keeping it to myself. Josie is my safe space, though. My one and only confidant.

"I can't believe you didn't tell me," she'd said, sounding a little hurt.

"I know. I'm sorry," I'd said. "I wanted to. It was . . . there was just so much. And then I didn't want to get everyone's hopes up about the money."

"And the sisters would not have understood."

I'd laughed at that. Josie knows this well, the misunderstandings our moms create. "No, they would have thought I was selling my body."

She'd laughed then, and we'd talked about all the ways the sisters would have misconstrued how I got the money.

"So why did you need to be talked down?" she'd asked, once we'd finished laughing about that.

"Because I might have developed feelings for him." It wasn't a *might* at this point. It was a full-blown thing.

"Oh, Jen."

I tsked. "I can see your teacher face through the phone."

"I *am* not—ugh, just get over it," she'd said, because clearly, I was right.

I sighed. "He's just like all the other guys I seem to attract. You'd all hate him. And honestly, I don't know if he's even attracted to me."

"He did take you to meet his mom," she'd said. "That's a pretty big deal."

"True. But he's not what I want. I want someone who's open and wants to tell me he has feelings for me. And not someone I have to pry every word out of. I'm so sick of that."

"I'm sorry," she'd said. "What do you want to do?"

"Maybe I can get him to insult our family again. That seemed to numb the attraction the first time."

She'd laughed again. "Shouldn't be too hard to get him to do that. Maybe invite him to closing night."

"Oh gosh." I'd felt sick just picturing that particular tradition. Us gathered around, singing that ridiculous song the sisters made up decades ago. "Not the song. That's the worst part."

"Worse than the ritualistic pumpkin chant we do at the beginning of the season?"

"It's all bad."

She'd sighed into the phone. "I'm sorry, Jen. I'd say your best bet is to hang in there. You're almost done helping him, right?"

"Yeah," I'd said. The thought of never seeing him again after his convention made me feel a little queasy.

"Well, get through that, and then maybe things will fall into place after."

"Or maybe we can find a magic spell that helps you stop having feelings for someone."

"Good idea. We'll ask the sisters for one."

"Thanks for listening," I'd said after she'd yawned and I'd realized we both needed to get up early the next morning.

"Love you, Jenna," she'd said as we were hanging up. "You've got this."

It's been three days, and I still don't "got" anything. I haven't seen Aidan since then, and we've only texted a bit because he's been so busy catching up with all the work he missed while he was in San Francisco.

I had hoped the distance would do me some good. But judging by how anxious I am to reply back to the text he just sent me, I'm clearly no better.

"What do we need to talk about?" I ask Chantelle just as Heather walks into the room.

"What are you two up to?" she asks. She's in light-blue scrubs and carrying a water bottle. A waft of a light floral perfume fills my nose as she comes over to the table. It's a smell I will probably always associate with her.

"Oh good, I'm glad you're here too," Chantelle tells her. They both take a seat at the table.

"Have you all noticed how different Mr. Hot Doctor's been acting lately?" Chantelle asks, getting down to business.

"This is what you wanted to talk about?" I ask her, confused. I've barely seen Dr. Shackwell in the past couple of weeks. Not since we had our little chat that he ran away from. He's only been at the spa a handful of days, since this is more of a part-time gig for him—his full-time job is at one of the clinics down the street. Except for a couple of pleasantries as we've passed one another, that's about all the interaction I've had with him.

"What do you mean, different?" Heather asks her.

"He was acting all strange when he was here last week doing Botox touch-ups. And then yesterday, the same."

"How so?" I ask, now slightly interested.

"He's just been quieter lately. And yesterday when I asked him how he was doing, do you know what he said?"

"Better now that you're here," Heather and I say at the same time.

"No!" She gives us wide eyes. "He said, 'I'm pretty good, thank you for asking.'" She lowers her tone, attempting to imitate Dr. Shackwell's voice. It was about as good as my Memphis accent.

"Well, that *is* different," Heather says. You can tell this isn't all that interesting to Heather, but she's trying to give it her best effort.

I'm fairly interested, though. Especially after the conversation he and I had. "Did you ask him if something's going on?"

"I didn't outright ask him. But I did tell him he was being weird."

"What did he say to that?" Heather asked.

"He just shrugged and said he had a lot on his mind."

"I wonder what that is?" I ask.

"I don't know, but I don't like it. I'm worried about the guy." She turns her gaze to Heather. "Maybe you should pray for him."

"I absolutely will," she says, with a grin.

"Why do you care so much?" I ask.

"Because I enjoy flirting on the days he's here. It's something different. It's boring around here otherwise."

"Gee, thanks," I say.

She bats my words away with her hand. "You know what I mean."

"Well, I'll leave it to you to get to the bottom of it," Heather says, getting up from her chair. "I've got a client coming in."

"Me too," I say, getting up from my seat. I don't have a client, but I also don't want to give Chantelle the chance to remember I'm hiding something from her. Because I am, and I also really want to know what the text from Aidan says.

Chapter Twenty-One

Jenna Peterson's Guide to Dating Emotionally Unavailable Men:

Last-minute plans are always on the agenda. Learn to be flexible.

It turns out when Aidan texted me yesterday, it was an invite to go sailing with him. I happened to have the afternoon off—after moving a couple of things around and begging Heather to take one of my appointments—so I told him yes.

And now I'm out on Aspen Lake, the water a beautiful inky-blue color and the mountains in the background giving off the light scent of pine in the air, with the clear blue sky above. The wind is in my hair, and I think I'm in love with *Carol*.

That's the name of Aidan's boat. He named it after his grandma. He's had it for a while now—one of his first adult purchases, so he told me. When I got my first paycheck from my first adult job, I was excited to buy myself one of those fancy coffee makers. So pretty much the same thing. And just like Aidan, I also named my coffee machine. I called it Al Cappuccino, even though it didn't actually make cappuccinos.

I wasn't sure what to wear for an outing like this since it's a cooler day as we move toward the end of October. Not big-winter-coat chilly, but enough to dress fairly warm. I'm wearing a pair of leggings with a cream oversized turtleneck sweater and a black-and-red life jacket to complete the look. Aidan's got on a matching life jacket, dark pants, and a high-collared white windbreaker jacket that fits him like a glove.

Other than the fact that I'm out on a sailboat on a Friday afternoon, things feel back to normal with Aidan. I'd wondered if Monday had meant as much to him as it did me, and if things would be different when I saw him again.

But we're back to our regularly scheduled programing: me asking him questions and him giving me short answers. Except for when I started asking him about the boat, and then that opened up a whole can of worms. Aidan knows a lot about this boat and a lot about sailing. It's like a foreign language to me. Terms like *heeling, tack, jibe,* and *jib*. Then he tried to tell me that a rope was called a sheet. And I accused him of just making crap up. Like, why not just call it a rope?

Then he got into the physics of the wind, and that's when I shut him down—politely of course—and told him to get on with the sailing part of this expedition already. I'm not down for a physics lesson on a Friday afternoon.

He chuckled and shook his head at me, and then, with his guidance, I helped him a bit as we got things going, and now we're out here sailing on the beautiful water of Aspen Lake. Just *Carol*, Aidan, and me.

We're quiet as Aidan steers the boat. It's windy, but not so much that we couldn't hear each other talk. But we're both quiet as we sail along. I find that I don't mind the silence like I usually do. It's nice to just be here with him.

"So, what do you think?" Aidan asks after a bit.

I look over at him. He's sitting across from me, steering the boat with something called a tiller. "It's amazing," I say. "I see why you love it."

The corners of his lips pull upward, that dimple on his cheek making an appearance. "Good," he says.

"Do you like to do any other kind of boating?"

"I sometimes take the speedboat out, but I mostly prefer this," he says. "What about you?"

"I've been on a few. This one guy I dated used to take me fishing."

Aidan's eyebrows move up his head. "Oh? Did you . . . did you like it?"

I smile with no teeth. "The fishing? No, not really."

I can't hear his chuckle over the sound of the wind, but I can see it by the look on his face and the way his shoulders shake.

"And the guy?" He keeps his eyes on the water in front of us.

"I didn't end up liking him either."

"Why?"

I lift my shoulders and let them drop. How do I answer this? Brian was emotionally unavailable, an alphahole, and he may or may not have cheated on me. "We weren't compatible" is all I tell him.

He frowns then. I'm not sure why.

"How about you tell me why Aspen Lake Boating Company should purchase a fleet of sailboats like this."

"Why?"

"For practice," I say. "For the conference you're going to?"

He shakes his head. "That's not really what I do. I'm just establishing relationships."

"But you'll have to talk business, won't you?"

"Maybe."

"So, try me."

He looks ahead at the water and then back at me. "Has anyone told you that you have a one-track mind?"

"I don't think I've ever been accused of that."

"I didn't bring you out here to work."

"Then why?"

He lifts a shoulder. "It was more of a thank-you," he says. Unwanted butterflies start. "For what?"

"Just everything," he says. "This past month, I've . . . It's . . . Well, it's been much needed."

"I'm glad," I say, giving him a big smile.

I think of what his mom said to me on Monday night—that I've been good for Aidan.

I hope so.

I watch Aidan tie the boat to the dock. The sun has almost set behind the mountains, and the breeze has gone from pleasant to bordering on bone chilling. I have his extra jacket draped over my shoulders, but it's not helping all that much.

"This was so amazing," I tell him as we start walking down the dock toward our parked cars.

"I'm glad you enjoyed it," he says, his voice sounding extra gruff. We're both a little hoarse from having to talk over the wind for so long.

"Well, speed dating might have been more fun, but we'll never know."

He chortles. "No, I suppose we never will."

"I'm still trying to figure out what else we can do. Have you been invited to any galas this weekend that you didn't tell me about?"

"Not that I know of."

"Hmmm," I say. "Any parties we could crash?"

"I'm not really into the party scene."

"You don't say," I reply, my voice sarcastic.

This makes him chuckle. "I don't see you as the party type either."

"I'll have you know I go to parties all the time," I say, trying to sound serious. "In fact, I have one on Sunday."

"What's that?"

I snort out a laugh. "It's the end-of-the-season party for the Peterson's Pumpkin Patch family and seasonal employees. Wanna be my plus-one?" I look over and wiggle my eyebrows at him. "That conference of yours will be a cakewalk compared to a Peterson party."

"Okay," he says.

This makes me stop in my tracks. Aidan gets a few steps ahead before realizing but then backs up to me.

"You can't be serious," I say.

He lifts a shoulder. "How bad could it be?"

I scoff. "Bad, Aidan. Even if I tell my family I'm bringing you as a friend, they won't believe it. They'll all think that you and I" — I point to him and then me — "are a thing."

"So?"

"So, you'd be inundated with questions."

"Isn't that exactly what I need to practice?"

I stop and stare at him, my mind rushing through thoughts and scenarios.

"I don't think — "

"Would it be as bad as speed dating?"

"Yes. One million times."

"Why?"

"Because these aren't random strangers, Aidan. This is my family. And we are fiercely protective of each other. To the point of insanity." The sisters were once on the news, holding up protest signs that said *Honk if you hate porn* in an attempt to save the children from the evils of HBO after Josie wrote her *Reece the Rogue Pirate* story.

He studies my face. "You said it was for employees too."

"Yes," I say.

"So it won't just be your family."

I let out a breath. "Yes, but that's not a buffer of any kind."

He reaches up and runs a finger down his jaw. "Aren't I technically an employee? I did work that one day. I even wore the beret."

I laugh as his lips curve upward. "That's true," I say. "But Aidan, you can't possibly want to go."

"Maybe . . . I'm curious," he says.

"Well, you know what they say about curiosity."

We're silent after that, the sound of the water hitting the dock in the distance and the wind rustling by, whipping through my hair.

I'm waiting for him to say never mind and that he's joking or something. Because this doesn't seem like Aidan, the quiet and reserved man I've come to know. For all the activities we've done, I've practically had to drag him to do each one.

He doesn't take it back, though. In fact, there's an earnestness in his gaze.

I attempt to put him off again. "You know you'll have to be pumpkiny, right? Like you'll have to wear something with a pumpkin on it. It's the dress code." Really, the sisters could have been much worse with this one—like required that we all dress as Priscilla Pumpkin.

"Do I have to wear the beret?" he asks.

"No," I say.

"Okay then. What time?"

"Are you serious?"

"I am."

I shake my head, chuckling. "I guess this would be the ultimate test to see if I've been able to help you at all. But a little more like throwing you into a den of lions."

"Will I leave with all my limbs?"

"Hopefully."

"Then . . . I'll be your plus-one."

Chapter Twenty-Two

Jenna Peterson's Guide to Dating Emotionally Unavailable Men:

Have low expectations if and when he meets your family. Like, bottom-of-the-sea level low. Because he's emotionally unavailable, chances are they won't like him and vice versa. Have an escape plan at the ready. Or some alcohol.

"Are you ready for this?" I ask Aidan as we walk down the path leading to my aunt and uncle's house. I reach up and touch the gold ring on my necklace. I'm going to need all the help I can get from Grandma Peterson tonight. Maybe she can send some Aidan's way as well.

"Sure," he says. He doesn't sound all that nervous, but I've got nerves enough for the both of us.

It's Sunday night, and I'm having regrets. I'd thought mostly of Aidan and how my family would react to him. But what about me? There'll be questions for me too.

At least Aidan delivered on the dress code. He's got on a pretty awful orange sweater with three rows of pumpkins knit into the center of it. As ugly as it is, it still somehow looks good on him.

For my part, I have on an orange slouchy sweatshirt with the black eyes and smiling mouth of a jack-o'-lantern in the center. It hangs off one shoulder, which gives it a little more style, as far as pumpkin attire goes, and also my mother will hate it. Maybe she'll focus more on that and not the man walking next to me right now. Wishful thinking.

Anxiousness swirls around in my belly as the lights of the red farmhouse with the wraparound porch come into view. This house has been a huge part of my life. I know all the secret spots and exactly where my aunt Lottie hides her stash of chocolate. Josie and I used to raid it during sleepovers.

My family is inside there, and no one knows I'm bringing Aidan. No one except Josie, that is. I texted her this morning to warn her. She thought I was crazy but then said she also kind of wants to meet the man that I've been spending so much time with. The one who's going to help save the barn.

"How are you going to introduce me?" Aidan asks as we walk toward the party. I can start to make out the low hum of people chatting and the drums and bass of some background music.

"I'm just going to tell them you're Aidan," I say.

"As in, like, 'my friend Aidan'?"

I shake my head. "Nope, just Aidan."

I look over to see he's got a confused look on his face. "Why?"

"Because it's better if you just let them make assumptions."

"Why's that?"

I let out a breath. "It won't matter what we tell them; if I bring you here with me, they'll think there's something happening between us. Especially my mom and my aunt. So, we're not going to give them any labels."

"So, am I supposed to pretend to be your date?"

This makes me stop walking, and Aidan stops too. I think about what he's just asked and then shake my head, remembering that he isn't good at pretending. "That's not necessary."

He turns to face me. "What if I don't mind?"

"Uh . . . be—being my date?" I say, stumbling over his words as I turn toward him.

"Won't I get the full Peterson effect if I am?" The side of his mouth lifts slightly.

"Well, yeah," I say, feeling a swarm of butterflies begin to fly around in my stomach at the thought of him being my date tonight. Even if it's not real.

"Then let's do that," he says.

"Are you sure? Because I don't know if you understand what you're getting yourself into. We're talking lots of questions. And possibly some over-the-top ones."

He pulls his brows inward. "Like what?"

"Oh, like what your future plans are, where you see yourself in five years. Stuff like that."

"That doesn't sound so bad."

"There will be more. It's a test, and they'll be judging you to see if you measure up. And I'll tell you that, so far, no one has."

"Measure up to what?"

"To be worthy of me," I say.

"That sounds like a good family to me," he says.

"You say that now."

As much as my family annoys me, it is something that they always have my back. None of them liked Matthew, Brian,

Garrett, or Cam. And I suppose they weren't wrong about them.

Aidan takes a step closer to me. He reaches out his hand toward me, palm up. I look down at it, and then back up at him.

I swallow. "What are you doing?"

"I'm getting ready for my debut," he says. "As your plus-one."

I shake my head at him, laughing. "This is crazy," I tell him.

"Let's go into the lion's den, then," he says, his eyebrows moving up his face, his hand still waiting for mine.

I place my hand in his, and my stomach flips as he weaves our fingers together.

And then we walk, hand in hand, into the Peterson's Pumpkin Patch party.

This is a dangerous game we're playing. Dangerous for me, at least. Aidan, the man who couldn't even role-play with me, is doing a hell of a job pretending we're together.

He's kept a hand on me pretty much the entire night so far, either holding mine, or resting his on my lower back, and sometimes if we're sitting, on my knee. I have to keep reminding myself it's all fake.

Not only that, but he's answered nearly every question fired at him from my family members. And in a way that is true to him. He's not overly animated or anything. He still uses the same gruff tone he always does, and his answers are short and to the point.

Like when my cousin Oliver asked him how well people who run a boat store do.

"Oliver, that's not appropriate," I'd said, my voice chastising. Even though I knew it was coming. It's the question Oliver always asks.

Aidan had just chuckled and said, "I do all right for myself."

It was the perfect answer, really. Humble, and not too much information. With the past boyfriends I've brought home, that line of questioning had always been awkward. Matthew, Garrett, and Cam had been overly offended by the question, and there was even a bit of an argument between Oliver and Matthew that heated up pretty quickly. Oliver's wife, Kitty, and I had to step in to stop it. As for Brian—he'd already been flexing his wealth, so he just flat out told him how much.

So far, my family doesn't seem to hate Aidan. Even Olivia hasn't given him the upturn of her perfect nose and has seemed pleased with the answers to her questions. Which are more of the *Where do you see yourself in five years?* variety. He told her he hoped to be further in his career and possibly married with a child or two. She liked that answer. So did my brain. The marquee board lit up again: *Marriage and kids! Marriage and kids!* I ignored it.

Josie is skeptical, of course. She knows the whole story, and she doesn't like the fake date thing, which she took me aside to ask about when Aidan and I first walked in holding hands.

Both she and Reece have been great buffers. They've helped us get out of conversations with Reginald the Pretentious, who somehow keeps trying to chat it up with Aidan. His questions are so ridiculous: "If Nietzsche and

208

Gandhi were in the same room, what do you think they'd talk about?"

He can't even ask a question that isn't pretentious.

But Aidan has taken it all in stride. We've yet to talk to the sisters, though. That'll be the true test for the work Aidan's done. They've been busy hanging out behind the island in the kitchen, where there's a large spread of food, talking and laughing with people as they dish up their famous pumpkin pie. I've gotten a few raised brows from my mom and my aunt when our eyes have met across the room. I know they're gearing up.

As for me . . . every minute we play up this fake date thing, another log is added to the fire of my attraction to this man. To Aidan. I like the way he touches me. I like it way too much. I feel a connection toward him, like maybe he likes it too.

And that scares me. Because despite how he's acting tonight, he's not the emotionally available type. I can't be with another man I have to make all the moves with and who never lets me know where I stand because he's not open enough to tell me, or in touch with his feelings enough to even know. And next time I give myself to someone, I want to know that we're headed for love—*real* love, whatever that is. I know how a relationship with someone like Aidan ends. And I wonder, especially in this case, if I'd be able to come back from a broken heart this time. Like a breakup with Aidan would be the thing that actually breaks me.

We're standing with Josie and Reece, after my dad finished his interrogation of Aidan—which wasn't much more than an introduction and a quick questioning eyebrow raise at me as he walked away (I love that man)—when Josie leans toward me and whispers, "Here they come."

I look over my shoulder to see the sisters walking toward Aidan and me, as we stand in my aunt Lottie's fall-decorated living room, their eyes laser-focused on us.

"Hello," my mom says as she approaches. "Jenna, are you going to introduce us?"

I take a breath. "Mom, Aunt Lottie . . . this is Aidan."

Chapter Twenty-Three

Jenna Peterson's Guide to Dating Emotionally Unavailable Men:

Confrontation will not be pleasant.

"That was exhausting," Aidan says as we walk toward the barn where we keep the tractors. I've been giving him a tour of the farm as an excuse to leave the party for a bit. He's seen it already, when he first came here, but I thought I'd show him where the barn that burned down used to be, and then we just kept walking.

"You did amazing," I tell him. And he did. He made it past all the questions the sisters fired at him. It was mostly my mom doing the asking, but Aunt Lottie would toss one in every once in a while. Some were along the same lines as some of the other members of my family, though nothing as forward as Oliver, because my mom would *never*. And there were definitely no pretentious questions like the ones from Reginald.

But they fired them off. Asking him everything from *Where are you from?* and *What kind of family did you grow up in?* to *What are your future plans?* and *How long have you been dating Jenna?*

That one was a little tricky since we'd never discussed it. But Aidan, the terrible liar that I thought he was, looked at me, instead of the sisters, and said, "She returned something to me that I'd lost a month ago, and I think I fell for her then."

It made my breath hitch in my chest. He seemed so serious when he said it, so intense. And for a second I wondered if it were true. *Pretending! Pretending!* The words rang in my head.

My mom seemed to be reserved but undoubtedly impressed. I fear for myself when she finds out this was all a sham. Because I'm sure she will. She's got her witchy ways, after all.

"This is the barn where we house the tractors," I say, giving him my best overexcited voice. It's totally fake, because who cares about tractors? A farm does, of course. It wouldn't function without them. And I'm sure Josie has a different opinion of them lately. Tractor rides have become a bit of a *thing* for her and Reece.

I slide open the door and we walk inside. I flip on the LED lights my dad and uncle installed years ago and walk over to the smaller utility tractor they were working on the other day. I touch the tall back wheel and think about the conversation I had with my dad. It's hard to believe it's been a week since we talked.

"You know, you have a pretty great family," he says to me while he looks around the barn.

I chortle. "I'm not sure about great," I say. Then I tilt my head at him, giving him a sassy look. "Do you take back all the mean things you said when we first met now?"

He gives me an annoyed look. "I've already apologized for that."

"You apologized, but you didn't take it back," I tease.

"I take it back," he says, holding his hands up, palms out toward me. "I see things a little differently now."

"Yes, you've had a front-row seat to the crazy."

"No, I just see the importance of your family traditions. They make you who you are."

"My mom and aunt are still loud, though."

"Yes, but it's more endearing now," he says.

"Wow, they've somehow pulled the wool over your eyes tonight," I say, and he chuckles.

"What's this?" Aidan asks, looking at a little four-by-six picture that's tacked up to one of the wooden posts near the entrance.

I walk over to him. "Oh, that's a picture of Olivia and me on my dad's lap on the opening day of the pumpkin patch." It's been hanging here for years, the picture fading in places, making it look older than it is.

"How old were you?"

"I think nine or ten?" I look at the picture, my dad with a big, toothy grin and Olivia and me in matching pigtails. Life was so much easier back then, even if I did complain about all the work we had to do around the farm. But that was the easy life, really. Being an adult is highly overrated. The little girl in that picture had no idea what was coming for her.

I glance to the side to see Aidan standing there. I turn fully toward him, liking the idea of being this close to him. Maybe I'll give him another hug. I've enjoyed pretending tonight. Too much, I know. But Later Today Jenna can deal with the emotional fallout from that.

I glance up to see Aidan looking at me, his blue eyes appearing grayer in the dim lighting of the barn.

I take a breath to steady myself and get a whiff of that woodsy and citrus cologne of his. Aidan's gaze is penetrating, as if he's trying to read my mind. "You did well tonight," I say, not wanting him to hear what my brain is actually saying right now, which is *Kiss him! Kiss him!* "I think you're ready for the conference."

"I think I'm much better. Thanks to you." He takes a tiny step toward me.

I swallow, attempting to ignore the way his proximity makes me feel. He's got a good seven inches of height on me, maybe more, and I don't know if I've ever realized that. Possibly because I've never been standing face-to-face with him, at least not this closely.

"You'll do great," I say, my voice slightly shaky.

He studies my face as he reaches up and tenderly pushes some strands of my hair back.

"Aidan," I say, my voice coming out as a whisper. "No one's around. We don't have to pretend anymore." I give him a little smile, my heart practically beating out of my chest.

"Who's pretending?"

He places a hand on my waist, his eyes dropping from the steady gaze he's been keeping on my eyes down to my mouth. His other hand comes up and cradles my cheek.

"What are you doing?" I reach up and grip his forearm to pull his hand away from my face, but instead I lean into him more, my hand around his arm anchoring me rather than pushing him away. I want him to kiss me. Aidan presses his fingers into my waist, and I move closer to him.

I hope he takes this as permission, but when he dips his head down, he lets his lips hover over mine, barely touching as our breaths mingle. I wonder if I'll have to close the distance, but then he slowly leans in and brushes his lips across mine. He pulls back slightly, hovering over my mouth again.

I let go of his forearm and wrap both my arms around his waist, pulling myself into him so there's no longer any space between us. His lips touch mine again; this time the pressure is harder.

I don't want him to pull back again. I don't think I can take it. So I open my mouth this time, and he takes full access of it, his hand moving away from my face and down my back as his lips move over mine. He sucks my bottom lip into his mouth and I let out a little moan, which has him suddenly pulling his lips away from mine.

He pulls his head back and we stare at each other, our breathing heavy. I should push him away. This isn't supposed to happen. But I don't want to just yet. I want more. I lean into him again.

He turns us so my back is facing the wall of the barn. He bends down and, wrapping his forearms around the backs of my upper thighs, he lifts me up, standing to his full height as he does. I wrap my legs around his waist in response, and he pushes us up against the wall for support. I stare into his eyes, now level with mine, and then grabbing his face in my hands, I kiss him.

It's not slow or tender like his first kisses. We go immediately back to where we left off. Our mouths moving over one another, his tongue dipping into my mouth and then running over my bottom lip.

Holy crap, Aidan St. Claire knows how to kiss. I'm dizzy with lust right now, my legs wrapped around him, our lips melding together.

Something scatters in the loft above us, causing us to jerk apart from the noise. The interruption knocks some sense back into me, and I'm shocked at how quickly this escalated. I unwrap my legs and pull out of his embrace, landing on my feet.

I touch my lips, confused.

"Aidan," I say, shaking my head. "We can't do this."

"Why?" He asks, pulling his brows inward.

"Because . . ." I stop talking, trying to find the words. *Because I like you too much? Because I want to keep kissing you? Because you aren't the kind of guy I want for myself?*

"Why?" he says again.

"Because you don't want this," I say.

"Yes, I do."

I shake my head. "You just got caught up in the pretending."

He furrows his brow. "Do you think I've been pretending all night?"

"Ha—haven't you?"

"What do you think? You've seen my role-playing skills." The corners of his lips move upward just slightly.

I close my eyes for a second. "Why didn't you say anything before? Why didn't you tell me?"

He sighs, taking a step toward me. "I told you I'm not good at that, at expressing myself."

He did tell me that when we first met. Which is why I told myself I couldn't like him. But then I went and liked him anyway. Oh, gosh. It wasn't just a dangerous game tonight— this whole month with Aidan has been dangerous. Despite all I've done to protect myself, my heart might break again.

I blink, and a tear falls down my cheek.

"Jenna," he says, putting a hand under my chin, gently directing my face upward to his. "Why are you crying?"

I pull away and back up from him. "This can't happen," I say. "I promised myself I'd do things differently the next time."

He scrunches his brow again. "What are you talking about?"

"I promised myself I wouldn't get involved with another emotionally unavailable man."

"Emotionally unavailable?" he repeats the words. "What's that supposed to mean?"

"You're emotionally unavailable, Aidan."

"No, I'm not."

"Not open, doesn't know how to express or show feelings." I start ticking items off on my fingers. I'm angry now, mostly at myself.

"I just showed you how I feel," he says, his arms at his sides, facing toward me like he's pleading his case.

"I have to be the one to initiate conversations with you." I'm still ticking things off.

"Jenna, what are you talking about?" he says, his voice getting louder. "I've done nothing but open up to you. I've been more open with you than anyone else in my life."

"That's because I know how to ask the right questions, to get people to talk. My *thing*? Remember?" Now my voice is getting louder.

He shakes his head, slowly. "Are you . . . serious? Jenna, if anyone is emotionally unavailable," he says, his tone low and intense, "it's you."

"What?"

"I've been trying to get to know you more; I've tried asking you questions. You've only given me bits of information and then change the subject back to me."

"That's because you're paying me to help you," I say.

He throws his head back, grumbling at the ceiling. "I did need your help, but that wasn't the only reason I asked for it."

"What are you talking about?"

He looks at me. "I . . . I wanted to spend time with you, to ask you out and then . . . then I insulted your family farm and I didn't know how to come back from that. I wanted to get to know you, Jenna. That's also why I asked you for help. But you never want to talk about you."

I stand there with my mouth open. He wanted to ask me out? He wanted to spend time with me?

I shake my head because I can't let that information take me off course. "You have no idea what you're talking about," I say. "I'm an open book. Just ask everyone in there." I point in the direction of the house where my family is, the party probably still going strong. And I'm in a barn listening to this gibberish from Aidan.

"I came to this party tonight just so I could learn about you, to see if maybe you'd be more forthcoming around your family. But no," he says. "I watched how you talked to everyone, and with each conversation, when someone asked you a question, you turned it back on them."

"I don't do that," I say.

"You do," he says flatly.

"I'm open," I say. "My heart is on my sleeve."

"Really? Then how do you feel about me?"

"I . . ."

"See? You can't do it."

"Yes, I can. I just need — "

"I can tell you how I feel about you." He puts his hands on his hips. "I don't know many of the small details, since you can hardly answer my questions. But what I do know about you is

218

that you're trustworthy. You're independent and fiercely loyal. You're perceptive, tenacious, you *never* give up. You also care about people almost to the detriment of yourself."

"I . . ." I swallow, but words won't seem to come out of my mouth.

"But I guess I'm too emotionally unavailable."

He stares at me for a second, and then he turns around and walks out the barn door.

Chapter Twenty-Four

Jenna Peterson's Guide to Dating Emotionally Unavailable Men:

When someone emotionally unavailable opens up to you, listen with your whole heart. It's a big deal.

I stay in that barn, sitting on that same utility tractor, for about an hour after Aidan walked out. My mind is a mess of thoughts, and it makes me sort of numb. But not numb enough to stop tears from falling down my face.

I keep replaying the look he gave me before he left. It was a look I'd never seen before. His lips pulled downward, the inner corners of his eyebrows raised, the way he blinked like he had to force himself instead of doing it instinctually. I hurt him.

I finally call Josie, who has already left the party with Reece.

"Jen, what's wrong?" she asks when she hears my snot-filled voice over the phone.

"Can I come stay at your place?" I ask. "I don't want to drive all the way home."

"Of course," she says. "I've got chocolate."

"Good," I say before hanging up.

I drag myself out of the barn and walk all the way back to the parking lot where I left my car earlier. Back when Aidan and I hadn't kissed or said all those things. That felt like a long time ago.

I drive to Josie's townhouse on autopilot and stumble up the steps to her door. She swings it open just as I was about to find the key to unlock it.

"Jenna," she says, her face cocked to the side.

"No teacher face," I say on a sob. Seeing her made the waterworks start up again. Then I take a step inside the door and let her wrap her arms around me as I cry into her shoulder.

"What's going on? Did something happen with Aidan?" she asks, rubbing my back.

"Yes," I say, my voice muffled into her shoulder.

"Come on," she says, patting me on the back. "Let's go sit down."

I pull out of the hug, and we move over to her living room. Josie's place is so welcoming. It's simple in decor—the opposite of how our moms decorate.

We sit on her couch, and just as she promised, the light-stained coffee table in front of us has a large spread of different kinds of chocolate. "You weren't kidding about the chocolate," I say.

"I might have a stash," she says.

"Well, I'm going to need it."

"What happened?"

"Aidan kissed me," I say.

"What?" Her eyes go wide. "Tell me everything."

"I mean, it was good. Really good," I tell her. "Up against the wall in the barn."

She covers her mouth with both hands and lets out a little squeal. "Are you serious?"

I nod my head. "But then . . ." I swallow, unsure how to explain what happened next. "I told him it was a mistake."

"Why?"

"Because he's emotionally unavailable."

She furrows her brow. "What do you mean?"

I take a breath. "It's not easy to explain."

She shakes her head, back and forth. "Don't give me that," she says. "What don't you want to tell me?"

I pull my brows downward. "What are you talking about?"

"You do that when you don't want to admit something to me. 'It's complicated,' 'I'll tell you later,' 'It's hard to explain' — they're all things you say when you don't want to talk about it."

I stare at her. "I don't do that. I'm an open book with you," I say.

She tilts her head to the side but then stops herself. "Except it took you weeks to admit what was going on with Aidan."

My shoulders drop and my mouth falls open. "I didn't know how to tell you. It was so strange."

"Not really," she says. "Unconventional, sure. But not all that weird."

"The Aidan thing was an exception," I tell her.

She shakes her head. "You hardly tell me about anyone you date. Unless you need my help with something."

"I do?" She nods. "I don't mean to do that."

She reaches over and touches my arm lightly. "It's okay, Jen. I know you. I'm here for whatever version of yourself you want to give me. So explain what happened with Aidan."

"Well, I guess it's kind of along the lines of what you just told me," I say, remembering what Chantelle said, and even

Olivia. I guess at the age of thirty, I'm still learning things about myself. Big things. Tears pool in the corners of my eyes, and I sniffle them back.

"How so?"

"I guess I need to go back a little further to explain."

So I tell her. I tell her about Matthew, Brian, Garrett, and Cam. About our different issues—most of which she already knew about—and how the one thing they had in common is that they were all some degree of emotionally unavailable.

"And you think Aidan is the same way?"

I nod my head at her. "It's my toxic trait. I attract emotionally unavailable men."

She smiles. "So then what happened with Aidan?"

I take a deep breath. "After we kissed—"

"Up against the barn wall," she says. "I thought tractor make outs were hot."

I chuckle. "I mean, as far as kisses go, it was in the top five. Possibly the very top spot."

"Okay, so after the kiss . . . ," she says, getting us back on track.

"Yes, so afterward, I told him it was a mistake."

"Oh," is all she says.

"And then I told him it was because he was emotionally unavailable and I can't be with someone like that again." I sniff away some burgeoning tears. "He was shocked, of course. But then he turned it on me. He said he's been trying to get to know me over this past month but I always give him quick answers and then turn it back on him."

"Right," Josie says, her face contemplative.

"Do I do that?"

"I mean . . ." She stops talking and then gives me a sheepish little smile with a quick raise of her shoulders.

I drop mine, letting my whole body sag. "Have I gotten this all wrong with him?"

"I don't know much about Aidan, but I'd say the other four definitely had issues."

I snort out a sad laugh at that. She always waited until after we broke up to tell me she didn't like them, but I could tell. I know my cousin well. She definitely wears her heart on her sleeve.

"But," she says, "maybe that's the kind of men you attract because it's something you recognize in yourself."

"Well, that was mean," I say, the tears pooling again.

"I'm sorry." She reaches up and rubs my arm softly. "So the question is, is Aidan really emotionally unavailable?"

"I don't know," I say. "I think I got it all wrong. Maybe he's more like reserved. Like it takes him a while to trust."

"That sounds a lot like you," she says, giving me a closed-mouth smile.

"I'm not—" I stop myself. I'm not reserved like Aidan, but apparently, I'm not the open book I thought I was. "What do I do? I insulted him. And after all those wonderful things he said about me. You should have seen his face when he left. He was so hurt." I'm crying now.

"What wonderful things did he say about you?" she asks, confusion on her face.

I tell her all the things Aidan said before he walked out. How I was trustworthy and tenacious and caring.

"Oh, wow," she says. "You need to fix this with him. I like him already."

"What if I do and he breaks my heart?"

"Is he worth the risk?"

Is he? That marquee board is back in my head, displaying a blinking *YES*.

"I think so?" I stammer. "I think . . . maybe I might love him."

I put my face in my hands because it's the first time I've said the words aloud, and I honestly don't know what love feels like—but this has to be it. This tugging sensation in my body, the pull I feel toward him. Like I belong with him. And the desperation I feel at the thought of it never happening.

"You need to tell him."

"How?"

She reaches over and pulls me into a hug. "I can't tell you that. And it won't be easy for you, Jen, being open like that. But I know you'll figure it out."

Chapter Twenty-Five

Jenna Peterson's Guide to Dating Emotionally Unavailable Men:

Finding out they were wrong is a difficult position to be in for someone who isn't in touch with their emotions. Be gentle.

The next day, I'm sitting in the break room looking at my phone, wondering if texting Aidan would be a good idea, when Dr. Shackwell walks in.

I think Josie's faith in me figuring out what to say to Aidan was misplaced. I have no idea what I should do.

"Hello," Dr. Shackwell says to me, a thin smile on his face.

"Hi, Dr. Shackwell," I say.

"You can call me Kal, you know," he says.

"Kal?" I'm not sure what I thought his first name would be, but that wasn't it.

"Yeah," he says drawing out the word. "Short for Kal-El." He gives me a knowing look.

My eyes go wide, which is probably the response he was expecting. "Like . . . Superman?"

"My parents were big fans," he says.

I wait for him to make a comment, something flirty or cocky, like, *It's because they knew I'd grow up to be a superhero with the chicks.* But he doesn't. He walks over to the small fridge and pulls out a soda.

It looks like he's just going to grab his drink and go, but he stops by the door. "You know what you said to me the other day? You pegged me. Perfectly."

"I hope it wasn't hurtful," I say.

He gives me a grin. "The truth always is, isn't it?"

I chortle. "It really is."

"It made me think, though. Is that really how I want people to see me?" He looks to the side and then back to me. "And I realized the answer is no. So, thank you for that."

"Well, I'm glad I could help," I say.

He starts to leave again. "Dr. Sha—Kal," I say, stopping him. "How . . . how would you peg me?"

That was the perfect opening for something flirty. I realized after I said it. But he doesn't take the bait. He studies my face for a few beats, before opening his mouth and saying, "I . . . well, I guess I wouldn't know. We haven't talked all that much about you. Maybe that was my bad. But also, you seem like the kind of person that doesn't like to talk about themselves."

I nod. "I think you may have hit that nail on the head."

His eyebrows move up his forehead. "Did I?"

"It's something I'm learning about myself," I say.

"That's not a bad thing, learning new things about yourself." He winks at me before walking out the door.

On Wednesday, I do something stupid. It's on a whim, because I was at home sitting on my pink couch overthinking everything. And I found myself wondering if any of the past men in my life know anything about me. Like, were those relationships just about me asking questions, getting them to talk, but never offering anything in return? I send Cam a message through Instagram asking him something personal about me. We dated for over a year; surely he remembers something.

Me: Hey, congrats on your upcoming nuptials. I wish you the best. Silly question, but do you remember what my favorite color is?

It's not long before I get a reply.

Cam: Hey! I hope you're able to make it. Would love you to be there. As for the color . . . I can't remember. I'm guessing red?

The guess is incorrect. That's actually *his* favorite color.

It's a dumb thing, and honestly, I'm not sure it's the best question to ask — it's been a while since we were together.

I decide to ask Olivia a different one.

Me: Dumb question: what's my favorite food?

Olivia: Why?

Me: Just humor me.

Olivia: Easy. It's Japanese.

Incorrect. That's her favorite food.

It's not that it matters whether people know these things about me — they don't make up who I am. The things Aidan saw in me . . . those are the things that matter. But if I'm not willing to talk about the small things, then I'm probably not talking about the big things either. What does that say about me?

I'm still thinking about this on Saturday as I stare at the donation jar on the counter. It's the end of the day and I need to count it, and I kind of don't want to.

I still haven't contacted Aidan. I don't know what I'd say to him. I keep hoping he'll text me and open up the conversation, but that hasn't happened either. I've probably hurt him beyond repair. That makes my heart actually ache in my chest.

The door to the office opens, and in walks my mom.

"Well," she says. "It's official. We won't make enough for the barn."

She flops down on one of the chairs.

That's the other thing—the money for the barn. It doesn't feel like Aidan to not come through on our deal, but it's also not something I can text him about either. *Hey, Aidan, I know I said some hurtful things to you and maybe misjudged you, but can I swing by and grab that check?*

"I'm sorry, Mom," I say.

"Well, we tried our best," she says.

"How far off were we?"

"Around fifteen thousand," she says.

"Oh," I say, slumping in my chair. Even if Aidan comes through, we still won't meet our goal.

"Will we have to sell some land?"

Her head snaps to me. "How did you know about that?"

"Olivia told me," I say.

She makes a scoffing noise. "She shouldn't be spreading that around."

"Is it true?"

She sighs. "We don't know yet."

"I'm sorry I couldn't come up with something to help. I thought I had something, but I don't think it will work out, or even be enough to help," I say. "Sorry to disappoint you . . . again."

She furrows her brow at me. "What do you mean, *again*?"

"Oh, you know." I bat the words away with a hand. "I'm just the family disappointment."

She lets out a little laugh. "No you're not," she says.

"But . . . what about the fact that I moved to Aspen Lake?"

"That doesn't disappoint me; I just want you closer because I want you here more."

"And my job?"

"I just thought you should be using the degree you worked so hard for, that's all. You can do what you want."

"What about the not married and no kids thing?" That one's sure to get her.

But instead she shakes her head. "I want you to be settled, of course. But I also want you to do it with the right person. Like . . . maybe that Aidan you brought to the party?"

That was a knife to the gut. I actually can feel a stabbing pain.

"That's probably not going to happen," I say.

She tilts her head. "Well, why not?"

"I think I messed it up."

"Well *un-mess* it," she says, like it's something easy to do, like a snap of the fingers. "He's the best thing you've ever brought home."

He really is the best thing I've brought home. I'm such an idiot.

"At least you have Olivia to give you all the things," I say.

She cackles—like, an actual witch-sounding laugh. "Olivia is a whole other story."

"What do you mean?"

"It's not my story to tell," she says. "But let's just say things aren't always as they seem."

"Really? Her perfect little life isn't so perfect?"

"Not even close," she says. "And even knowing that, I'm not disappointed in her either. That's honestly a feeling I've never had for either of my beautiful girls."

She stands up and walks over to me. Leaning down, she places a kiss on the top of my head.

"Thanks, Mom," I say.

She starts to walk out the door but I stop her. "Hey, dumb question."

"There are no dumb questions."

"What's my favorite color?"

"I stand corrected: that is dumb." She gives me a broad smile; she's teasing me. She reaches up and taps her chin with her finger. "You know, I don't know what your current one is, but your favorite growing up was violet."

I smile. She's not wrong. That was my favorite color. It was all over my room.

She goes to open the door. "One more thing," I say, stopping her.

"If you had to pick, what's your favorite quality of mine?"

"That's easy. Your determination. You got that from me," she says, pride in her tone.

"Dad would call that stubbornness."

"Same thing."

"Thanks, Mom," I say, smiling.

"Anytime," she says. "And sit up, Jenna. You're slouching."

With that, she opens the door and leaves.

Chapter Twenty-Six

Jenna Peterson's Guide to Dating Emotionally Unavailable Men:

If you hang on, someone who's emotionally unavailable
may start to come around. But remember: real change
happens from within.

Halloween comes the following weekend. That means
closing day for the pumpkin patch season and more crazy
traditions from the Peterson family. Our normal patrons are
gone for the day, and then after the little ceremony the sisters
make us do every year, the farm opens up for a special night of
trick-or-treating. But I won't be here for that.

That's because when we're done here, I'm going to talk to
Aidan. I almost want to skip the whole thing with my family,
but I know how important this is to them. Especially the sisters.

I'm sick to my stomach with nerves, thinking about going
to see him. Even my grandma's gold band isn't bringing me
comfort. I don't know exactly what I'm going to say, but I'm
going to try. The plan is to go to his house—I'm hoping he's
home since I doubt he's out partying it up for Halloween—and
knock on his door and tell him whatever comes to me. I know

there will be apologizing, maybe some groveling. And I'm not above begging.

I take a breath and look around at the Peterson family and employees gathered in a circle where the old barn used to be. The sisters are in the center, as always. Smiling as they look around. I look over at Josie, who's holding hands with Reece, and his little daughter, Andi, next to them. They look like a perfect little family standing there. Josie gives me a little head shake, like, *Here we go*. I can't believe she was daring enough to bring them to this.

It makes me briefly wonder what it would be like to have Aidan here next to me, sharing this crazy part of my family with him. I can see it perfectly, him watching us all with that scowl on his face. The thought makes me smile.

I look over to see Olivia and her family next to her—Reginald and my niece and nephews, all dressed to perfection and standing properly. It's funny, but since my mom mentioned that things weren't always as they seemed with Olivia, I've noticed certain things. Like the look of exhaustion that crosses her features every once in a while. Or the way she sometimes glares at Reginald when he's not looking. I sort of see her in a different light now, and it makes me want to get to know my sister better. Like maybe we have more in common than either of us thinks we do.

"We did it," the sisters yell at the same time, bringing everyone's attention to them.

Aunt Lottie lets out a little sigh. "We just wanted to thank everyone for all their hard work this year. We couldn't have done it without you."

"We also wanted to let you know," my mom says, her voice wobbling slightly, "we fell short on donations, but . . ."

She puffs up her chest, ready to say something profound and hopeful.

"Wait," Josie says, interrupting her. I glance over to see her looking at the sisters. "I have a last-minute anonymous donation."

What? Did Reece donate more money? Why didn't she tell me?

"From whom?" Aunt Lottie asks.

"I said anonymous," Josie says, her eyebrows raised.

She reaches into her pocket and walks over to the sisters carrying some sort of folded-up paper in her hand. She hands it to my mom, who opens up the check, and then both she and Lottie immediately burst into tears.

However much it is, it must have been a significant amount, because the sisters are dancing around now and then jumping up and down like they're in high school. My dad and uncle walk over, both smiling and shaking their heads.

I give Josie a look as she walks back to the circle, letting her know with one quick lift of my eyebrows that she's going to spill who the donor is. She gives me a quick nod like she's planning on it.

Once my mom and aunt get themselves under control, after all the crying and jumping, they both take a breath and then, in unison—like a couple of witches—they say, "It's time."

They hum a note for us and then begin to lead us in a very pumpkiny song. Well, it's to the tune of "Jingle Bell Rock," so that kind of makes it less so. The lyrics are silly—I think we even say *hayride* twice. But, it's our song, and it's part of our tradition.

Unfortunately, when they were kids, the sisters had once won a Christmas talent show by singing the original song. They kept the dance moves to it, which they expect us all to do while singing this new version. Even though it wouldn't be the same without them, I die a little inside each time we perform them. I briefly wonder who's going to take over all this gibberish when the sisters are too old. Josie and me? I cringe a little at the thought.

But I lift my leg when I'm supposed to and clap my hands and spin around as we sing the little ditty.

Peterson's! Peterson's! family-owned farm
Pumpkins and corn
And hayrides and more
Cider and mazes and hayrides too
Look what the Petersons have for you!

Peterson's! Peterson's! family-owned farm
The season is done
And the pumpkins all gone
We'll see you next year, so don't be too blue
Peterson's is here for you!

What a fun time, is the fall time
To visit us at the farm
'Cause the fall time is the best time
To see everyone arm in arm.

Peterson's! Peterson's! family-owned farm
Come back next year, oh please
We'll be here, just wait and see
Because that's the Petersons'
That's the Petersons'
That's the Petersons' farm!

I smile and laugh with everyone when it's done. I look over at Josie, who's laughing with Reece and Andi. She locks eyes with me and then whispers something to Reece.

She comes over to me. "Hey, you," she says, a bright smile still on her face.

"You're looking very *happy family* over there," I say.

"I . . . hope so," she says, giving me a sly grin.

"Wait, are you guys talking the m-word?"

She gives me a quick little nod. "Nothing in stone, but it's been tossed around."

I hug her. "That's the best news."

She takes a breath after we separate. "So, the anonymous donor," she begins.

"Oh yeah, who was it?"

She looks me in the eyes. "It was Aidan."

"What?" I say to her, my mouth falling open. "Did he drop off the five thousand to you?"

She shakes her head, slowly. "He got Reece's number the other night at the party."

I knew that. The two of them hit it off and Aidan had even mentioned going golfing with him, which was a huge thing for him to do, even though Reece wouldn't know that.

"He asked Reece for my number and then called me to see if he could bring me the money."

"Oh," I say, feeling my heart drop into my stomach. He went through a lot of trouble to get that check to the farm without having to see me. He didn't *want* to see me. Well, that makes what I was going to do tonight obsolete, I guess.

"Jen," she says, reaching over and touching my arm. "He wanted to know the full amount needed for the barn."

"Why?"

"Because that's how much he wrote the check for."

"What?" I say, tears springing to my eyes. "Why?"

"He didn't say, and he told me not to tell you, but you know I can't keep that from you. I think you should go talk to him."

"I wanted to. I was planning on it," I say, tears running down my cheeks. Why would Aidan do such a thing? *Because he's a good man and you're an idiot*, my brain tells me.

"Then do it," she says.

"But I don't know if he wants to see me, and now if I go running over there, he'll think it's because of the money."

I drop my head, the tears coming faster now. How did I mess this up so badly?

"Just go talk to him," she says. "You have to try."

I sniffle, knowing she's right.

"And you should do it right now," she says, nodding her head at me. "Like, right *right* now."

I laugh and give her another hug. "Love you," I say.

"You, too."

Then I leave her and my family and run to the office to grab my things.

It feels like it takes me forever to get to Aidan's house.

When I get to the gate and punch in the code—the one he gave me the one and only time I've been here—and it works, I punch the roof of my car triumphantly. I wasn't sure how I'd get in here, and I didn't know if he'd answer a text asking for the code again. I figured in the worst case scenario I'd climb the fence if I had to, but luckily that's not necessary.

I park the car in the driveway and get out. As I walk to the door, I take some steadying breaths of the cold, pine-scented night air. I touch the gold band on my necklace. *Help me to not screw this up, Grandma Peterson.*

I can see a dim light coming through the semi-opaque glass on the door as I approach. Before I can talk myself out of it, I ring the doorbell.

It's only a few seconds until I can see a shadow walking toward me.

The door opens, and there stands Aidan in a forest-green sweater and jeans, his feet bare.

"Jenna?"

"Trick or treat," I say, since it's Halloween and all.

He doesn't smile. "Josie told you," he says.

"Yes," I say. "And I can't believe you did that, Aidan. Why?"

"I wanted to," he says simply. "You didn't need to come all this way to thank me."

"That's not why I came." I shake my head at him. "I mean, I do thank you. You have no idea what this means to my family and me. But I'd planned to come here before Josie told me."

This gets his attention. "Why?'

"Because I wanted to tell you some things."

"Okay," he says, giving me a curt nod like he wants to get this over with.

I let out a breath. "My favorite color is mint green." He furrows his brow at this, but I continue. "And I hate coconut — *any* kind of coconut — with a passion."

"That's . . . uh — " I stop him with the palm of my hand.

"I only like to watch rom-coms, or anything with Chris Hemsworth in it. I hate it when someone is walking slowly in front of me—people traffic is the worst." I take a breath and then continue. "I get twitchy when it's silent, or when my phone battery goes below twenty percent."

Aidan is staring at me now, the scowl gone.

"I hate that I hurt you, and that I was so . . . so wrong about you," I choke up on the words, my eyes filling with tears. "I want you to know every little thing about me. I want to share it all with you. And I—"

"I love you," he says, cutting me off.

I blink my eyes at him. "What?"

"I'm in love with you."

I start crying fully now. I'm so grateful none of the other men I've dated ever said those words to me, because the way Aidan just said it, with that look of deep admiration in his eyes, is the only way I want to remember hearing those three words for the first time.

"And I love you," I tell him.

He takes a step out the door and pulls me into him, wrapping his arms around me. Then his lips find mine, and he's not gentle or light at all. His kisses are fervent and passionate, like he's making up for lost time.

He stops to pull back and look at me, and we smile at each other. Then he bends down and lifts me up, and I wrap my legs around him, just like that night in the barn. I grab his face, placing kisses all over it, like I can't get enough of him. Because I can't. I'll never get enough of Aidan St. Claire.

Epilogue

Two and a half months later

"What are you thinking about?" I ask as we sit on the massive gray couch in Aidan's living room, curled up together in the corner. The gas fireplace is on, and the snow has been falling outside for hours. We're supposed to get three feet tonight.

I look over to see the corners of his lips pull upward. "Just that I'm glad you're here."

I smile at him. "Really?"

He nods.

"You know, you've gotten really cheesy since we started dating." This is a lie, of course; getting Aidan to open up can still sometimes be like trying to get water from a cactus, but we've made some big strides in that area.

Likewise, I've been better about not changing the subject when the conversation turns to me. Actually, I've taken to that so well, I sometimes wonder if Aidan misses the old me. He usually just kisses me to shut me up. I know what he's doing and it works every time.

One thing's for sure: this relationship has been nothing like any I've been in before. I know where I stand with Aidan at all times, we spend a lot of time with each other's families — mine is still a little too much for him, but I think he's adjusting — and talk of the future often. The m-word has even been brought up more than once. I don't fear heartbreak with Aidan; in fact, I feel quite the opposite. My heart has been put back together by being with him.

Next week we're taking our relationship to the next level . . . we're traveling together. We're going to get out of the frigid cold that is Aspen Lake during the winter and go on a weeklong trip to Cabo. There happens to be a wedding there I was invited to all the way back in September. I never thought I'd want to go, but when I brought it up to Aidan, he said it was a great excuse to see me in a bikini.

Relationships aren't perfect — I know this. Arguments happen, and feelings get hurt. But the one between Aidan and me is the real deal, and it feels pretty perfect to me.

THE END

Want to read Josie's story? Check out
A PUMPKIN AND A PATCH
on Amazon!

About The Author

Becky Monson is a mother of three and a wife to one but would ditch them all for Henry Cavill. She used to write at night but now she's too dang tired, so she fits in writing between driving kids around to activities and running a household. With a talent for procrastination, Becky finds if she doesn't watch herself, she can waste an entire afternoon binge-watching Netflix. She's a USA Today bestseller and an award-winning author, and when she does actually get off Netflix to write, she uses humor and true life experiences to bring her characters to life.

Becky wishes she had a British accent and a magic spell to do her laundry. She has been trying to give up Diet Coke for the past ten years but has failed miserably.

www.beckymonson.com

Made in the USA
Middletown, DE
11 August 2024